T[

EDEN PARK
KILLER

An enthralling murder mystery with a twist

FRANCES LLOYD

DI Jack Dawes Mystery Series Book 11

Joffe Books, London
www.joffebooks.com

First published in Great Britain in 2023

Cover art by Dee Dee Book Covers

ISBN: 978-1-83526-237-5

CHAPTER ONE

Tom Broadbent was a dead man walking. He'd known it the minute he'd triggered the alarm. The Eden Park security guards spotted him and raced after him, baying like a pack of hounds. He ran — of course he did — skidding and sliding on the snow-covered pavement. They chased him as far as the perimeter gates, but he was fit and could outrun the clumsy goons, hired for muscle rather than speed. Fitness was essential in his line of business. So was meticulous planning.

He escaped the same way he got in — through a concealed gap he'd made in one of the fences. But he had no illusions. CCTV was on every corner of this exclusive, protected environment. He'd been able to dodge the cameras when he broke in but now, in a desperate dash to get away, his face would have shown up on all the monitors. They would hunt him down, and after what he'd seen, there would be no stay of execution, no let-off with a warning to keep his mouth shut. He'd had a tip that the house would be empty or he'd never have risked breaking in. Something had gone badly wrong. His only hope now — and it was a slim one — was to get out of the country, but that would take time and money and he had precious little of either. In the meantime,

1

he needed somewhere safe to hide — and someone he could trust to help him.

* * *

Kings Richington is an affluent and rapidly growing market town. It sits beside a quiet stretch of the Thames, biding its time until someone considers it important enough to make it a city. Its portmanteau name derives from the nearby urbanised developments of Kingston, Richmond and Teddington and has little to do with any royal association, although local historians believe "Kings" was added in 1830 as a homage to the accession of the benevolent William IV over his dissolute elder brother, George IV.

Among the villages, shopping centres and housing estates lies the gated development of Eden Park. Well-kept lawns and neatly trimmed shrubs preserve the soothing aesthetic of a secluded haven. It isn't unique. There are more than a thousand similar communities in England. Demand for voluntary segregation from the rest of society is growing, particularly among young professionals attracted by the prestige of an upmarket address. Older residents who are fearful of the escalating city crime, seek comfort in the security of a patrolled environment. Here, in Eden Park, are the millionaire mansions of the seriously wealthy — investment bankers, industrialists, racing drivers and media influencers — and among that eclectic bunch — one ruthless and very powerful crime boss.

To his neighbours, Bernie Shakespeare was an affable and respected member of the Eden Park community. He lived with his Sicilian wife, Teresa, and two grown-up sons, Jonnie and Marco, who helped to run his ostensibly successful logistics business. Most people, including His Majesty's Revenue & Customs, assumed that it was the cash generated by this legitimate company that sustained his lavish lifestyle. He was an active and generous supporter of many local charities and on a summer afternoon, he would exchange his bespoke Savile Row suit for a white coat and could be seen on the village green, umpiring the Kings Richington cricket match.

In reality, he was a violent and dangerous member of the underworld. Shakespeare's nickname in gangland was "The Bard", and he was revered and feared in equal measure. Despite being a vicious criminal, he had assumed some kind of celebrity status and was unchallenged by rival gang leaders who considered him too big to bring down. He owned several nightclubs in the city, whimsically named after Shakespeare's plays, and not so whimsically, all registered in his wife's name for a variety of nefarious business reasons. It was in The Tempest Club, the most overtly respectable of these establishments, that he regularly provided hospitality to politicians, senior police officers, judges and anybody else who might be useful to him.

Behind this facade of respectability, Bernie considered torture, murder, armed robbery, arson, protection rackets, drug-trafficking and prostitution, to be the acceptable tools of his trade. It was into the elegant home of this formidable perpetrator of organized crime that Tom Broadbent — petty thief and failed burglar — had recklessly stumbled.

* * *

Snow fell silently but relentlessly that night as it had for most of the day. The Kings Richington landscape, never one of nature's most picturesque creations, was now shrouded in a crisp and sparkling mantle. In Eden Park, a white blanket covered trees, gardens and houses. The residents turned up the heating and the security guards turned up their collars.

Tom sprinted back to the stolen van he'd left hidden down a side road outside the gates. He'd intended to use it to make his getaway with burgled loot, then torch it somewhere out of town. But he was too late — he spotted one of Bernie's men already watching it. He knew he dared not go home to his shabby bedsit in the next town — that was the first place they'd look for him. Instead, he traipsed the streets, a scarf obscuring his face, and searched for somewhere warm where he could hide and decide what to do next. It was late and the only place open was a takeaway — Corrie's Kitchen. He loitered outside until everyone inside had left and the place was empty. The girl serving was tidying up, as if she was about to close. After a quick look to make sure no one was watching, he pushed open the door and hurried inside.

She smiled. 'You look frozen. How about some hot soup? I've got cream of tomato, minestrone and I think there's some mulligatawny left. It's been very popular tonight. It's the curry, you see. Warms you up.'

Tom peered at the blackboard menu on the wall. He'd come out with only a handful of loose change. His modus operandi was simple — he broke into people's houses while they were out and helped himself to their cash and valuables. This time of year, there were expensive gifts under their Christmas trees that he could flog later down the market. He didn't need to take money with him. Almost all the posh houses in Eden Park had sophisticated burglar alarms in addition to the security patrols. They were smart systems, Wi-Fi controlled, but he'd learned to hack in and disable them during technology classes in prison. Briefly, he wondered about overpowering the girl behind the counter and raiding the till. But it was only briefly. He'd never used violence in the past and didn't intend to start now. 'I'll just have a burger, if that's OK.'

'Certainly.' The staff had gone, anxious to get home before the buses stopped running, so she cooked it herself. She put two burgers and a pile of onions in the bun and added a few chips. It was almost closing time and the poor bloke looked frozen. She glanced at him. He was scrawny, at least fifty, she reckoned, and he wore just black jeans, a scarf and a thin, dark hoodie, not the right clothes for this kind of weather. It would never have occurred to her that this was the preferred mode of dress for a burglar needing to move swiftly and unobtrusively. It wasn't the stereotypical striped jersey, black eye mask and a bag with "swag" on it, but it served the same purpose. She handed him the food. 'Do you want to eat it in here rather than take it out in the cold? I don't expect any more customers tonight.'

'Yes, please.'

'Would you like a mug of tea?'

He felt in his pocket and pulled out a handful of change. He looked doubtful. 'I'm not sure I've got enough for tea.'

'Don't worry. It's on the house. I was going to have one myself, anyway.'

'Thanks.' He bit into his burger and chewed, all the while glancing around furtively. 'What's your name?'

'Carlene.'

'Is this your place?'

She shook her head. 'No, it's an outlet of Coriander's Cuisine. It's a very successful catering company. I own a Michelin-starred bistro at the other end of town.' She was proud of Chez Carlene. Hard work and inspired cookery had resulted in a successful and lucrative enterprise, which she ran with her French chef partner, Antoine. 'I'm helping out here because the usual assistant has gone down with flu.'

Tom turned to read the sign that was painted on the shop front in big green letters — Corrie's Kitchen. He pointed. 'Is he the owner?'

'Yes, except Corrie is a "she". It's short for Coriander.' She studied his expression. 'You're not from round here, are you?'

'Not really.' He had no intention of giving her any personal information but his mind was working fast. It couldn't be, could it? Too much of a coincidence. But Coriander was a most unusual name. He'd only ever met one lady with that name before. 'What's Corrie's surname?'

'Dawes. You seem very interested. Do you know her?'

'Dunno. I might do. What was her name before that?'

Carlene frowned. 'I've no idea. Why?'

He picked up a paper napkin. 'You got a pen?'

She handed him one from the counter, wondering if she should ask him to leave. He didn't seem at all the type to be a friend of Mrs D's. Growing up in a local authority children's home, Corrie was the closest Carlene had ever had to a real mother and she loved her dearly. Her protective instincts kicked in. What did this unkempt and dodgy-looking bloke want with her?

'Thanks for the burger and tea, love.' He scribbled something on the napkin. 'Could you give this to Corrie?' He handed it over. Pulling up his hood and scarf, he pushed open the door and trudged out into the snow. The way he saw it, this could be the break he was looking for. Even if he'd got it wrong, he'd be no worse off. If she wasn't *his* Coriander, she'd just write him off as a nutter and chuck the napkin away.

Outside, everything was quiet. All he could hear was the sound of his trainers crunching in the snow. He reckoned he was getting too old for this lark. Time he packed it in. But then, what else would he do? Nobody would employ him with his prison record. By the time he entered the underpass, he was feeling slightly more positive. If this woman *was* Coriander — his Coriander, the woman that he hoped she was — she would help him to get away, wouldn't she? Although they had parted under less than convivial circumstances, they had been painfully young and there had been no real animosity. All he needed was somewhere to lie low for a while until he could arrange a flight abroad. Somewhere warm. Spain, maybe? No, not Spain. Bernie Shakespeare might still have contacts there, old associates he'd done business with in the past, now holed up on the Costa del Crime with new identities. No, it would need to be further away than Spain . . .

Tom stopped in his tracks. A flickering light had appeared at the end of the underpass. In the shadows, two figures were sprinting towards him. He turned to run but there were two more heavies behind him, blocking his escape. He was caught in a trap. As they drew closer, he recognized Marco Shakespeare, Bernie's younger son. He had a reputation for mindless violence that was equal to that of his father, if not worse. No point in trying to escape and taking a beating, Tom decided. He doubted they'd risk killing him here, so he'd go

6

quietly in the hope of giving them the slip later. They grabbed him, bending him forward and wrenching his arms up behind his back. Marco pulled out his phone and called his father.

'We've got him, Papà. What do you want us to do with him?'

Bernie's voice was barely audible over the music, laughter and loud chatter in the background. 'We're still in the Tempest Club where you should have been,' he shouted, 'then none of this would have happened. Take him to the house and keep him there until I get home. I want to find out how much he thinks he saw. Don't do anything stupid, Marco. You've caused enough trouble for one night.' He ended the call.

* * *

Jonnie got up from his seat down the far end of the table and came to sit beside his father. 'Is everything all right, Dad? You look flushed. Remember what the medics said about your heart.'

Bernie thought, not for the first time, how lucky he was to have a son like Jonnie. He thought strategically, kept his head under pressure and was the right person to have on your side in a dangerous situation. And when he took over the syndicate, there would be plenty of those.

'Yes, I'm fine, son. It's your brother. He's got himself into a bit of trouble.'

'Do you want me to go and sort him out?'

'No, you stay here and enjoy the party. It's time he learned to deal with his own mistakes.'

'Why isn't Marco here, anyway? It's your birthday. He should be here with the family. He promised Mother he would come.'

'Marco had an . . . accident . . . earlier. He needs time to deal with the fallout. Don't worry, Jonnie.' He squeezed his arm. 'It'll be fine.'

* * *

7

The guards manhandled Tom back down the tunnel. A car with blacked-out windows was waiting with the engine running and they bundled him into it. He was wedged in the back between two hefty brutes and had an idea that he might try to reason with them, more in hope than expectation. They didn't look like reasonable men. 'Look, guys, I know you think I'm a loose cannon, but I'm not a grass. Let me go and I swear that's the last you'll see of me. I'll disappear abroad, somewhere the filth will never find me. What d'you say?'

'Shuddup!'

When they reached the Eden Park gates, the security guard recognized the boss's Bentley with the heavily tinted windows, and waved it through. The car purred through the snow-covered estate until it slithered quietly to a halt outside the Shakespeares' mansion. The muscle-bound minder beside Tom pushed open the door and clambered out. He turned to drag Tom after him but hit a patch of snow-covered ice. His feet shot out from under him and he fell heavily, sprawling backwards onto the drive. This was Tom's chance and he didn't hesitate. He scrambled through the open door and ran as fast as he could. He knew his way around the estate, even in the dark, having carefully cased it before attempting the burglary.

Clearly, he couldn't escape through the main gates which were heavily guarded, so he headed for the gap in the fence that he'd made earlier that evening. He crawled through and was out into the lane that ran alongside the rear of the residents' gardens. Fifty yards, a hundred at most, and he'd be away from Eden Park and thumbing a lift from one of the overnight lorries on the main road out of town. He took a deep, steadying breath, thinking he was home free. Then he heard rustling in the bushes, saw the brief flash of a blade and felt a sharp blow between his shoulder blades. He staggered for a few moments then collapsed face down in the snow, a knife sticking out of his back.

* * *

'I had to waste him, Papà. He was trying to get away. The body's lying in some bushes.' Marco was back on his phone, his voice shaky despite his feigned bravado. 'I had no choice. What he saw would have put me inside for a long time.' He gulped. 'Even Gregory couldn't get me off this one. I'd be looking at life. What shall I do?'

Sir Gregory Munro was a top-class barrister whose brilliant histrionics in court had enabled several of Bernie's enforcers to avoid the lengthy prison sentences they deserved. Gregory had a penchant for rough sex — a partiality that was catered for by the club's specialist call girls on a quid pro quo basis, anonymity guaranteed. It was an arrangement that suited both barrister and gangster and the sex workers, who were paid double.

This time, Bernie got up from the table and went upstairs to the club's office so he wouldn't be overheard. His tone was harsh. 'Marco, what were you thinking? Why didn't you just let the guys take him back to the house to be dealt with?' He spoke more calmly. 'You know what you have to do, now. Get rid of the body and anything that could be traced back to you or the organization.' Bernie was trying to remember which of his men had gone with Marco. They all valued their jobs because their dubious credentials would make it nigh on impossible to get another one, so he knew they would make sure the boss's son didn't do anything stupid. 'Watch out for the cameras. I'll make sure all Eden Park's CCTV is disabled when you get back home. That way, if anyone asks, you can say you were at the club all night celebrating my birthday. Everyone here will confirm it. Keep your head and don't panic.'

He terminated the call, with Marco still asking desperate questions on the other end, and went back to the table where Teresa had ordered a cake and champagne to toast his birthday. Bernie loved both his sons and looked forward to a peaceful retirement with Teresa, after they took over the syndicate. He believed he'd taught them everything he knew. Jonnie was sound, steady and a safe pair of hands

— destined to fill the shoes of The Bard. Marco was the exact opposite — handsome, charismatic and hot-blooded. He was his mother's favourite and had inherited Teresa's striking Sicilian good looks — olive complexion, a shock of black hair and dark, flashing eyes. He also had her volatile temperament. He acted first, often in an uncontrolled rage, then panicked about the consequences when it was too late. Bernie had instructed Grant, his right-hand man, minder and chief enforcer, to clean up after Marco's first blunder of the night. This second one was up to Marco himself to sort out. It would teach him a lesson for the future although Bernie doubted Marco would ever have the balls or intelligence to run the firm. It would be down to Jonnie to carry on the Shakespeare dynasty. Half an hour later, when Bernie was ordering another bottle of champagne, Grant appeared.

'Evening, boss. Happy birthday.'

'Good evening, Grant. Sit down and have a glass of champagne.' He spoke quietly. 'Did you sort out that little problem, like I asked?'

Grant nodded. 'Yes, boss. All done.'

'I take it there won't be any unpleasant repercussions.'

'Definitely not, boss. I got some help from a guy who owes us a favour.'

'And you're sure this guy will keep his mouth shut?'

'Hundred per cent. He knows his health depends on it.'

'I hope the "problem" won't resurface when we least expect it.'

'Nothing for you to worry about, boss. The problem is hidden where nobody will find it for a very long time.'

'Good man. Help yourself to a piece of cake.'

* * *

There was blood in the snow — a great deal of blood. Claret red on pure white, the contrast was stark. Maurice could see it from the bedroom window as he was getting ready for bed. He was one of the less wealthy residents of Eden Park and lived in one of the smaller houses, built to fill a gap at the end of the development and close to the main road. A confirmed bachelor, he had moved there after he retired from running Kings Richington Post Office. Without a job to go to, he'd found himself at something of a loose end. Often, the high spot of his day was discovering that the local supermarket was offering three-for-two on loo rolls and he'd end up buying enough to last all year, barring any unforeseen bouts of dysentery.

In search of an interesting hobby, he'd developed a keen interest in wildlife and decided the blood was probably from some unfortunate creature killed by a predator. Murder right there in the lane outside his back garden. What was the saying? Nature red in tooth and claw? He was getting fanciful in his old age. He doubted it would just be a mouse killed by one of the many big cats that hunted there, yowling and growling. Some nights it was like the plains of the Serengeti. Similarly, there was far too much blood for the resident sparrowhawk to have dispatched a hapless dove. Too much even for a fox to have slaughtered a rabbit.

He was sure the blood hadn't been there when Coriander's Cuisine had delivered his dinner earlier that evening. He'd treated himself to the meal for the weekend — his favourite steak and kidney pudding. It sounded ordinary but Corrie's steak and kidney pud was to die for. As it was her last delivery of the evening, she'd stayed for a cup of tea and a chat. They'd discussed recipes — things he could cook for himself — and she'd made him a list of useful ingredients. Such a kind lady, spending all that time with him when she must have been exhausted. After she'd gone and he'd demolished his supper, he didn't feel much like sleep, so he went downstairs and out into the garden in his dressing gown to have a closer look at the blood.

It appeared to him that a large animal had been killed there and the carcass dragged for a short distance. Then the trails of blood suddenly stopped, as if it had been picked up and carried off.

CHAPTER TWO

Corrie Dawes was exhausted. Coriander's Cuisine was always busy at this time of year but even so, she'd had a lot more deliveries than usual that evening. She guessed it was a combination of bad weather — folk not wanting to drive to a restaurant through the snow — and the approaching festivities. People were in the mood for entertaining and needed to make sure they had enough goodies stored away, in case friends popped in unexpectedly. Her catering business, "superb Christmas food delivered straight to your door — just heat and eat" was the perfect solution.

On her phone's playlist, Michael Bublé was claiming that "it was beginning to look a lot like Christmas" and tree lights twinkled in the bay windows of many houses. But not on the Eden Park estate. Such ostentation was considered vulgar by the residents who confined themselves to a tasteful holly wreath on the front door. Not for them the strings of flashing icicles and an inflated, oversized Santa Claus, swaying in the front garden. Corrie did a good deal of trade in this gated community. People here were prepared to spend large sums on her quality dinner party and luncheon menus, not just for themselves but to impress their friends without any effort on their part. In that neighbourhood, it was important to make the right impression. Corrie delivered the food in appropriately elegant serving dishes then went back next day to collect the empties. The security guards on the gate were used to her bright-green van with the Cuisine's logo on the side, coming and going at all hours, and waved her in and out without the usual menacing interrogation.

After she left Maurice, Corrie plodded through the snow to where she had parked her van. She was looking forward to a late supper and her nice warm bed. The dream evaporated when she discovered the lock on the door of her van had frozen. With no other means of thawing it, she had to breathe hard on it for several minutes before she could open the door. Dizzy from near hyperventilation, she stumbled into the driving seat only to find the windscreen was totally iced up. She clambered back out with her scraper and took time to clear it properly. She had seen folk driving with just a tiny square to peer through which terrified her, thinking that without peripheral vision, some small inoffensive creature might dive in from the slips and get squashed.

Finally, with lifeless hands, she crawled back in, anxious to get moving and start the heater before she froze to death. The van, like its owner, was not in the first flush of youth and as a protest at being left out in the snow, refused to start. After several attempts, Corrie decided she'd have to phone the breakdown people to whom she paid squillions of dosh but had never used. It was then she discovered that her phone's battery was flat. She blamed Michael Bublé. She was cold, tired and irritable.

'OK,' she said out loud to the van, 'this is your last chance. If you don't start this time, it's the scrapyard for you.' The threat worked. The engine fired up and she drove away quickly before it changed its mind.

It was past one o'clock when she finally pulled up outside the ever-expanding industrial unit that was the beating heart of Coriander's Cuisine — or that was how she liked to think of it. It was on the outskirts of Kings Richington so she still had a twenty-minute drive home in her car before she could relax. She decided just to lock the van inside the garage and unload it in the morning. There was nothing in it that demanded her immediate attention, just empty dishes, kitchen equipment and leftovers. The roads were icy and hazardous, with broken-down cars and other abandoned vehicles along the route, so the journey took longer than usual. Finally, she let herself into her warm, welcoming kitchen where her husband Jack had prepared a late supper. As a detective inspector in the police service, he was used to working late nights himself, so the rule was, whoever got home first cooked some food. His repertoire was limited, mostly dishes based on mince, but right now she could have eaten a dead horse between two mouldy loaves.

'Hello, darling.' He got up to kiss her. 'I've made cottage pie.' He lifted a steaming dish from the oven and spooned it onto plates, while she hung up her coat and kicked off her shoes. He poured her a glass of wine from a bottle that had already taken a significant hit while he'd been cooking. Some of it had even found its way into the food. 'Long day, but I'm guessing business is good.'

'Yep. I'm not complaining. How about you?' Corrie picked up a fork.

'Not much in. Looks like folk are delaying bumping each other off until after Christmas.' The Murder Investigation Team, of which Jack was the head, was filling its time with paperwork, and he knew they would relish a murder to investigate even though the victim obviously wouldn't. He had warned the team: 'Be careful what you wish for. Murders, like buses, often come two at a time.'

There was a tap on the back door and Carlene poked her head round. It was unusual for her to visit so late.

'Hey, Carlene. D'you want some cottage pie?' Jack fetched another plate. 'I realize it's a bit downmarket for a chef with a Michelin Star, but it's perfectly edible.

'No thanks, I won't stop, Inspector Jack.' Carlene had called him by this affectionate name ever since they had taken her under their roof several years ago, from the local authority half-way house. She had been sent there when she got too old for the children's home. 'I just thought I'd drop this in for Mrs D on my way back.'

Carlene now shared a flat with her boyfriend, Antoine, whose parents owned a chain of French restaurants. They frequently worked together and regularly swapped recipes. She handed over the folded napkin bearing the scribbled message.

Corrie took it, smiling. 'Well, this is mysterious. What do I want with a greasy napkin smelling of onions? Is it a surprise?'

'Dunno. Might be. A customer in the takeaway tonight wrote a message on it and asked me to give it to you. He was a weird old bloke — sort of skinny and shabby. He was on edge the whole time he was eating his burger — kept looking at the door as if he was expecting someone. Anyway, he reckoned he might know you, so I thought I'd bring it ASAP.' She picked up a fork and helped herself to a large mouthful of cottage pie from Jack's plate. 'Not bad, Inspector Jack. Could do with a tad more thyme.'

He grinned at her. Funny how chefs, especially good ones, were always hungry. He had a brief flashback of her aged sixteen, studs through her eyebrows, tormented magenta hair and cropped tops that exposed a complicated tattoo on her stomach not unlike a map of the London Underground. She had come such a long way since those days and he and Corrie were very proud of her.

Curious, Corrie unfolded the napkin. 'I don't think I know any weird, skinny, shabby old blokes, apart from Chief Superintendent Garwood, but—' She stopped abruptly when she read: *Andie, I'm in trouble and I need somewhere to hide. Please help me, for old times' sake.* Carlene and Jack looked at her expectantly, but she said nothing for several moments and her expression was hard to read. Memories came flooding back into Corrie's head. Only one person had ever called her Andie. Tom Broadbent — her ex-husband. He suffered from a particularly severe form of rhotacism, the speech impediment which meant he couldn't pronounce 'r'. He found "Corrie" more or less impossible, and "Coriander" wasn't much better, so he had abbreviated her name to the more manageable "Andie". She had neither seen nor heard from him in well over twenty years — so why now? Surely it couldn't have been him in the takeaway, could it? She turned to Carlene. 'Where did this man go after you closed up?'

'I didn't really see. I know he didn't have a car because I remember thinking he wasn't dressed for plodding through the snow. He made off in the direction of the underpass. Tell you one thing I remember, though. He had a funny way of talking. When he said "really" it came out as "weally" — like that presenter bloke on the telly who does chat shows.'

Corrie was convinced now that the man had, in fact, been Tom. But what was he doing in Kings Richington and why was he looking for her after all this time? And what kind of trouble was he in? Should she even care, after what he did? She made a sudden decision, and screwing up the napkin, she chucked it in the bin.

Jack and Carlene exchanged glances but didn't comment. It was Corrie's note and if she'd wanted to share it with them, she would have.

'Right. I'll . . . er . . . push off and leave you to your supper.' Carlene helped herself to a last forkful of Jack's food, hugged them both and trudged off through the snow to her car.

* * *

After Corrie had gone up to have her shower before bed, Jack sat at the table and poured himself the last of the Merlot. He stared at the bin. Ten minutes later, he realized he was still staring at it. He and Corrie trusted each other totally. They had no secrets. They shared all aspects of their lives — good and bad. It would be breaking that trust if he opened the bin, took out the napkin and read the message. Worse, even, than reading the emails on her phone, and he'd never do that. He'd heard that prying on that scale could end your marriage or at the very least, earn you a clout round the ear. On the other hand, whatever it was had certainly disturbed her — that much was obvious.

His conscience goaded him. What if she'd got herself into some kind of jam but was too embarrassed to ask him for help? It wouldn't be the first time she'd got embroiled in a dangerous situation, mostly on the pretext of "helping" him with a case. If he took a quick look, he reasoned, it wouldn't be an invasion of Corrie's privacy, it would be a duty of care for his much-loved wife. And he was a copper, after all. If there was some creep out there stalking women, it was up to him to put a stop to it. If it turned out to be nothing — just some crank commenting on her food — then he could forget about it and there'd be no harm done. He stood up, walked purposefully towards the bin and was about to open it when Corrie came back, towelling her hair.

'Your turn for the shower, sweetheart. I'll bring you up a hot drink before bed.' Jack had no choice but to go upstairs.

* * *

Next morning, Jack waited until after Corrie had left for work, then he searched through the bin. The napkin had gone. Jack was puzzled. *Why had Corrie retrieved it? It was obviously more important than she'd wanted to admit.* His thoughts were interrupted by a shrill rendition of "Mission Impossible" from his phone. Carlene had put on the distinctive ringtone because she said it would help him to distinguish between work calls and private ones. It always made him jump.

'Morning, guv.' It was his deputy, Detective Sergeant Malone, known predictably to his colleagues as Bugsy. 'We need you out at Richington Cross. Uniform have been called out to a body. A young woman.'

Jack reached for his coat and grabbed his car keys. From what he could remember, Richington Cross was mainly farmland with a scattering of smallholdings. 'Don't tell me — she was found by an intrepid dog walker or some fitness

fanatic, running through the snow in her vest and knickers.'
That was the usual scenario.

'Not this time, Jack. A farmer found her early this morning, under the tyres and tarpaulin on top of his silage.'

'OK, Bugsy. Secure the scene. I'm on my way.'

* * *

The pathologist, Dr Veronica Hardacre, known affectionately as Big Ron due to her larger-than-life persona, was already at the scene with her team of SOCOs, when Jack arrived. She and her diminutive assistant, Marigold Catwater, both dressed in full protective suits, were perched precariously on top of the mound of silage. The farmer had initially removed some of the car tyres and tarpaulin to get at the food for his cows. Uniformed officers had removed the rest to facilitate access to the body. There was no way they could erect a forensics tent so they were having to work out in the open.

'Morning, Doctor Hardacre. Are you all right up there?' Jack called.

'I've been better,' she shouted down. 'It's bloody cold.'

'What have we got?'

'Why don't you come up and see for yourself, Inspector? Don't walk in those footprints.' She indicated two sets of boot prints in the silage, on one side of the mound. Down below, a member of the SOCO team was waiting patiently to make casts but without much enthusiasm. She had never made casts in silage before and it looked too friable to obtain any kind of result that could be used as evidence, but she'd give it a go.

Jack fetched wellington boots from the car and he and Bugsy clambered up, their feet sinking into the brown fodder.

Doctor Hardacre was bent over the corpse. 'She's female, somewhere between eighteen and twenty, slim build, blonde hair, wearing expensive silk pyjamas but no underwear. Indentations show that she was accustomed to wearing jewellery, but it's been removed, even her earrings — could be robbery or to delay identification. She was wrapped in this blanket.' She indicated a cheap, grey blanket of the kind used by removal firms to protect furniture. 'You can buy them anywhere, I imagine, but that's your part of the job.'

'Does she have any kind of ID on her at all? What happened to her phone?' asked Bugsy, innocently.

Doctor Hardacre gave him a withering look. 'Funnily enough, Sergeant, despite the omnipresence of smartphones among the public in general and the younger generation in particular, not many of them feel the need to carry one in their pyjamas. No, we don't have any ID yet, but she's young so no doubt someone will report her missing, if they haven't already done so.'

'Any sign of . . .' began Jack.

'No obvious sexual interference as far as I can see, Inspector, but I'll do a thorough examination when I get her back to the mortuary. She didn't die here, of course. My initial opinion is that time of death was between ten o'clock last night and two this morning, and that she was carried up here and concealed soon after. Rigor mortis is complete so probably around midnight.'

'Cause of death, Doc?' Bugsy asked tentatively. He'd often been on the receiving end of Big Ron's sharp tongue for asking "bloody silly" questions before she was ready to answer them. This time she had no doubt.

'Death was by strangulation. I'd say it was manual. No indication of a ligature, but there are incipient pressure marks and some scratches on her neck. I'll know more after the post-mortem. Shall we say two o'clock this afternoon?'

She yelled to the mortuary men down below. 'You can take her away now, gentlemen. Please be careful.' She started the precarious descent, slithering down the silage and holding on to Miss Catwater for support.

'Where's the farmer who found the body?' Jack asked the constable who was securing the area which was cordoned off by blue police tape.

'Over there, sir. Gave him a bit of a turn, by all accounts.'

19

Bert Cook was sitting inside his battered Land Rover for warmth, drinking hot, sweet tea from a flask, brought out to him from the farmhouse by his wife. He was anxious to explain how he had found the young lady but equally anxious to assure the police — and his wife — that he had no idea who she was, nor how her body came to be on top of his silage.

'It was sheer luck that I found her when I did, Inspector.' He realized what he'd said. 'Beg pardon. Luck's the wrong word. I mean, it wasn't lucky for the young lady, was it? You see, normally, I wouldn't have accessed that particular silage for another six months at least. It can keep for a couple of years, longer if necessary. But due to the bad weather this winter, I brought my beasts inside earlier than usual and they needed extra food. So did my neighbours' cows and I'd planned to sell them some of my silage. I could tell that someone or something had already disturbed the snow on the tarpaulin, but I thought nothing of it at the time, believing it to be foxes or badgers. I certainly didn't expect to find a body underneath.' He shuddered.

'And you've never seen the young lady before?' asked Bugsy.

'No, never. Obviously, I didn't stand there staring at her body, poor little soul. I came back down sharpish and told the wife. She rang your people straightaway.'

'Do you want to take another look at her, just to make sure?' Bugsy asked.

'No . . . no, I don't! Once was more than enough.'

'Who else works on the farm, Mr Cook?' asked Jack. 'I'm assuming you don't manage it alone.'

Bert took another gulp of tea. 'Fred, my farm manager, works for me full time. He's been with me coming up ten years now. Solid and dependable. Couldn't ask for a better worker. Don't know how I'd manage without him. Then there's young Darren who helps out with the milking. He's only been with me a year or so, after he came out of prison. He's the wife's sister's neighbour's boy. She said he was trying to go straight and needed a job so I thought I'd give him a chance.'

'Is he any good?' asked Bugsy.

'The cows seem to like him. That's all that matters really.'

'Anybody else?'

'Well, I hire extra hands from time to time, when I need them. Seasonal work. Servicing the equipment. That sort of thing.'

'We'll need a list of everyone you've employed for the last couple of years, please, with their contact details,' said Jack.

'Oh. Right. Well, the wife does the books, wages, national insurance and all that. She'll give you their names and addresses.'

'How easy would it be for someone to get onto your premises at night?' Bugsy wanted to know.

Bert thought about it. 'Well, very easy, I suppose. Obviously, all the farm machinery and anything else of value is locked up at night and you'd need the keys, but you could get into the fields and the yard just by driving through the gates.

'Doctor Hardacre said the deceased wasn't killed here, so her body must have been transported in something,' said Bugsy. He had been hoping for tyre tracks in the snow but it had already been churned to slush by the comings and goings of all the other vehicles. The ground underneath was rock hard, so not much help there.

'Why here? Why me?' asked Bert, plaintively. 'I don't understand. Why would anybody murder a lovely young woman, just starting out in life, then bring her body here and hide it under my tarpaulin? It doesn't make any sense.'

'That's what we're going to find out,' promised Jack. 'Thanks for your help, Mr Cook. We'll be in touch.'

* * *

'What d'you reckon, Bugsy?' asked Jack. They were in Jack's car on the way back to the station. 'Does Cook know more than he's letting on?'

'I very much doubt it, guv. He was genuinely shocked. When uniform first got there, they found him throwing up in a corner of the field.'

'Not a case of a bit of extra-marital gone wrong, then?'

'Definitely not. Did you see his wife? Any hanky-panky and she'd chew him up and spit out the pips.'

'OK. Well, hopefully, we'll have more to go on, once we identify the body.'

CHAPTER THREE

In the incident room of Kings Richington MIT, DC Aled Williams was setting up the whiteboard. Apart from a photograph of the deceased and a map of the farm and surrounding land, it was a bit sparse. The team, including Clive, the digital forensic specialist, had been doing some digging.

'How far have you got with tracing the other farm workers?' asked Jack.

DC Gemma Fox looked at her screen, where she had been compiling background information. 'Fred Lynch is a full-time agricultural worker who has been with Cook for ten years. He lives in a semi in Richington Barrow with a wife, Jean, and two children. Darren Fletcher is the young chap who comes in to help with the milking.'

'Do we have anything that might connect either of them to the crime?' asked Bugsy.

'Nothing conclusive yet.' Clive tapped away. 'The full-time worker is clean but the lad who helps with the milking has form. He's a bit of a tearaway — started off at fourteen, nicking cars, then progressed to Class B drugs. He's had a couple of spells inside, mainly for the cannabis offences. Possession and dealing.'

'Doesn't make him a murderer, though, does it?' muttered Aled.

'Has anyone reported the dead girl missing?' asked DC Velma Dinkley. As a psychology graduate, Velma looked more closely into the neurodiversity of suspects and their victims, which made her a valuable member of the team, especially when it came to profiling. Velma wasn't her real name. It was what Scooby Doo fans at university had called her and it had stuck, much to her mother's disappointment. She'd named her Beatrice from *Much Ado About Nothing* as an icon of female empowerment, although it could be argued that Velma Dinkley had a similar role in the cartoon.

'Not yet,' said Clive. 'It's too soon for her to be a MISPER. Her family, or whoever she lives with, might just be assuming she stayed over with a friend after a night out. She was wearing pyjamas, so she obviously wasn't intending to go home.'

'Yes, but what if she already *was* home,' argued Velma, 'and someone in her home killed her? Most murder victims are killed by someone they know. Unlike in horror films, very few are killed by calculated, psychopathic strangers. Statistics show that the most dangerous place for a woman to be, where she is most at risk of being assaulted or murdered, is in her own home.'

Gemma pulled a face. 'Thanks for that, Velma. I'll remember it when I get home in the dark and let myself into the flat that I've always believed to be my safe place — until now.'

Jack intervened. 'I think we must conclude that whoever dumped her under that tarpaulin didn't expect the body to be discovered until after most of the evidence had been compromised, at least long enough to make identification difficult. Bert Cook said silage can sometimes be left undisturbed for at least a couple of years. The killer wasn't expecting her to be found just a few hours later, so that gives us a bit of an advantage.'

'In that case,' said Gemma, 'who else, apart from Farmer Cook, would know enough about silage to take a chance that it wouldn't be needed for a long time and would remain intact?'

'OK', said Jack, who had been thinking along the same lines himself, 'locate the farm workers and we'll see what they can tell us.'

* * *

Corrie had left home for the Cuisine earlier than usual that morning. Crawling through the already congested traffic, she was still distracted by the note which had kept her awake most of the night. Twice she'd got up and creeped downstairs to the kitchen to make tea, trying to avoid disturbing Jack, who was snoring raucously. She had rescued Tom's note from the bin and put it in her handbag, planning to destroy it later.

The traffic lights turned red and she sat, wondering how many other women's ex-husbands turned up out of the blue after decades, asking for help. On her playlist, Michael Bublé had given way to Sir Elton, who was "stepping into Christmas" but she wasn't really listening. Even if she did feel disposed to help Tom — and she wasn't sure she did — she had no way of getting in contact with him. There had been no address or mobile number on the napkin. By the time she reached work, she decided that she'd fretted over the issue long enough and it didn't deserve any more of her time. If Tom turned up in person, she'd think again.

The small car park was already full of vehicles belonging to her co-workers, keen to get a head start on the day's preparations. As soon as Corrie went through the door, Joyce, her head supervisor, called out, 'Mrs Dawes, do you know where the large cake stand is? I can't find it and the mayor has asked for a hundred mince pies for the civic Christmas bash. I thought they'd look good piled up in rows with sprigs of holly.'

Business always took priority. Corrie snapped out of her mental meanderings and returned swiftly to the present. 'Sorry, Joyce, I've got it. It's in the back of the van. It was too late to unload it last night, but I'll go and do it now.' Lady

Lobelia, wife of Commander Sir Barnaby Featherstonehaugh, had ordered a cascade of Christmas cupcakes for her Charity Ladies' annual shindig and Corrie had called to collect the dishes and the cake stand. The bins outside had been full of Prosecco bottles so Corrie reckoned it must have been a good party. Now, she trudged back outside, through the snow which was beginning to fall in earnest. Surely this year there would be a white Christmas. She made a mental note to ensure they had enough turkeys, cakes and puddings prepared, ready for the inevitable last-minute rush of orders when people found they couldn't get to the shops.

Unlocking the garage, she went inside, released the rear doors of her recalcitrant van and flung them wide open. Corrie was not given to hysterical outbursts. Things like spiders and mice, even snakes, did not bother her in the least and it wasn't as if she hadn't been through some scary moments over the years. She'd been poisoned by a psychotic botanist, bashed unconscious with a ballroom dancing trophy, held hostage on the parapet of an eighty-foot tower and half-drowned in a lake of Chardonnay, but none of that came even close to the shock facing her now. She leaped back several paces and let out an involuntary scream, loud enough to be overheard by the cooks in the kitchen. Immediately, several of them ran out to see what was wrong.

'Are you all right, Mrs Dawes?'

Corrie slammed the van doors shut before anyone could see what was inside and swiftly handed over the cake stand that she'd managed to grab hold of.

'Er . . . yes . . .' she stammered. 'I'm fine. I . . . er . . . just shut my finger in the van door.'

'Is it broken?'

'No, the door's fine . . . I just opened it awkwardly . . . Oh, I see what you mean. No, I don't think my finger's broken.' Corrie could hear herself babbling, mindlessly. It was the shock. 'Look. I can still move it.' She wagged a finger at them to prove it.

'Is it bleeding? Shall I get the first-aid kit?'

'No . . . thank you. I'll be absolutely fine. I'm sorry I made such a fuss. Please don't stand out here in the cold.'

Unconvinced, they shuffled back inside, muttering to one another. This wasn't like Mrs Dawes. She never over-re-acted. She'd barely flinched that time the tea urn exploded during the Bowls Club finger buffet. And when they'd found a live gerbil behind the radiator during a Food Standards inspection, she'd calmly trapped it in a cake box and smug-gled it outside. No, she definitely wasn't prone to panic. This must be something really serious.

After they'd gone, Corrie locked herself inside the garage and took a deep breath. She opened the van doors just a chink and peered inside. No, she hadn't imagined it. It was still there — a man's body, face down in a bowl of leftover trifle with one of her vegetable knives sticking out of his back.

She gave herself a stern talking-to. *Now, get a grip, Corrie, and try to think clearly. The garage and the van have been locked securely overnight. Nobody has broken in. So, the logical assumption is that the body was already in there when you drove home.* She recoiled at the hygiene implications of a corpse in a food delivery situation. Goodness only knew what those nice inspectors from the Food Standards Agency would make of it, but she had a pretty good idea!

That meant someone had shoved it in there at some point after her last delivery, which was Maurice's steak and kidney pudding. She had stayed chatting to the old gentle-man while the van was parked nearby and hadn't opened the doors again until just now. Eventually, shock gave way to indignation. *What a blooming cheek! Some low-life nicks one of my knives, stabs some poor soul with it, then to add insult to injury, dumps the body in my van!*

Well, she hadn't been married to a police detective for the last ten years without learning anything. This was a crime scene now, and she mustn't touch anything until after Big Ron and the team had processed it. There was only one thing to do — phone Jack. Then she paused . . . no, that would look like she was expecting special treatment because she was his wife. After all, she reasoned, when you came right down to it, she was in a slightly tricky situation. Her van had a murdered man in it, stabbed with a knife that was undeniably hers. She didn't want accusations of a conspiracy to cover up her potential involvement. She needed to be investigated properly and cleared of any suspicion, like every other member of the public who finds a dead person in the back of their vehicle. She would go through the proper channels. She locked the van and went inside to her office to phone the station.

* * *

Norman Parsloe had been desk sergeant at Richington nick for more years than he cared to remember. He was, effectively, the filter between members of the public with genuine concerns and those who, for whatever reason, sought to waste police time. Or as Bugsy put it, Norman operated the "nutter alert". When Mrs Dawes came through, he assumed it was a personal call to Jack and she hadn't been able to get him on his mobile.

'Morning, Mrs Dawes. Hang on a minute and I'll put you through to the DI.'

'No, don't do that, Norman. I'm ringing as an ordinary member of the public to report a dead body.'

'Dear me, you haven't poisoned another one, have you?' He chuckled at his feeble joke.

'No, I'm serious. When I opened up my van this morning, there was a dead body in the back.'

'Blimey!' He paused, processing this information. 'Are you sure it isn't a shop window dummy or something, put there as a practical joke? It's that time of year when boozed-up idiots who think they're funny decide to play silly buggers. It's not wearing a Santa Claus outfit, is it?'

Corrie supressed an impatient groan. 'I'm quite sure, Norman. It's definitely a dead body and it isn't dressed as Santa Claus.'

'Do you know who it is?'

'Not a clue. I can't see his face — it's buried in trifle. What's the normal procedure in a case like this?'

'Well, I haven't dealt with many cases where the corpse's face was buried in trifle, but first I'd ask you for your name and address. As I already know it, we can skip that bit. Then I'd ask how you found the deceased, and you've just told me. Then I'd tell you to stay put and not touch anything and I'd send someone from uniform to collect information about the circumstances of the death. They would check the body and note the presence of any injury.'

'Well, that's easy. He's got one of my vegetable knives sticking out of his back.'

'I see. Well then, I'd relay this to the MIT. Then the DI and Sergeant Malone would attend to ensure there are no issues of concern surrounding the death.'

'OK, well let's just do it according to the book, shall we?'

'All right, Mrs Dawes, if that's the way you want it.' Privately, Sergeant Parsloe thought it would be quicker if she just told Jack herself, but after she'd ended the call, he rang through to the MIT room like she wanted.

Sergeant Malone answered. 'Watcha, Norman, my old woodentop. What can we do for you?'

'Hello, Bugsy. I've just had a concerned member of the public on the blower. I think you and Jack need to hear this.'

'Is this going to take long? Only I've just bought a pie from the canteen and I don't want my suet crust going limp.'

'Seriously, Bugsy, this is more important than food.'

'Norman, mate, that's where you've been going wrong. Nothing's more important than food. Try going without for a few weeks and you'll see what I mean.'

'Jack will definitely be interested in what this lady told me.'

'OK, Norman. I've put you on speaker so Jack can hear. Fire away.'

Norman cleared his throat. 'The lady phoned to report finding a body in the back of her vehicle this morning. She reckoned it'd been there all night.'

'How does she know that?' asked Jack. 'Sounds a bit eccentric. Have you sent a couple of uniforms to check it out?'

Norman hesitated. 'Normally I would, Jack, but I thought you'd rather go yourself. I know this lady and she's well-respected. I'm sure she's telling the truth.'

Bugsy snorted. 'That's what you said about that lady magistrate they arrested in the Co-op. Turned out she had two pounds of frozen mince and a custard tart down her knickers.'

'I know,' grumbled Norman. 'No logic to it at all. Now, if it had been two pounds of fillet steak, I might have understood. But this is different. Jack, the lady on the phone was your wife.'

'What!' Jack jumped out of his chair and shouted into the phone. 'Why didn't you put her through?'

'She didn't want me to — said she wanted to follow normal procedure. I expect she was worried we might think she was asking for preferential treatment.'

'OK. Thanks, Norman. I'm on my way.' Jack grabbed his coat and shouted to the team. 'Can you T.I.E. the farm workers connected with the silage murder, please?'

Trace, Interview and Eliminate enquiries were one of the cornerstones of most homicide and major incident investigations, and familiar practice to the detective constables who sprang into action. 'We're on it, sir.'

Jack hurried to the door, wondering what on earth Corrie had been up to this time. 'Bugsy, you're with me.'

CHAPTER FOUR

Jack scrunched the car to a halt in Coriander's Cuisine car park and jumped out. Bugsy was hot on his heels. He pushed through the doors of the catering unit and called abruptly to one of the young cooks. 'Where's Mrs Dawes?'

'Hello, Inspector Dawes.' The young cook was surprised. Something was definitely up. She knew Mrs Dawes' husband was a police detective and rarely visited during the day. You could tell he was upset. Not so much as a "Good Morning". It wasn't like him at all. Such a charmer, usually, and quite good looking for his age. 'I haven't seen her for a while. I believe she's back in the garage.'

It was bitterly cold. He and Bugsy crunched through the snow to the garage and Jack tried the doors. They were locked. He banged on them. 'Corrie, are you in there?'

The doors opened a smidgeon and she peered out, sheepishly. 'Hello, Jack. Hello, Bugsy. You'd better come in.'

They squeezed through the crack. 'What's this all about, Corrie?' Jack was worried. He never knew for certain what she was up to and she'd got herself mixed up in some seriously dangerous scrapes in the past. 'Norman says you phoned the station and said something about finding a body in your van.'

'That's right. Look for yourself.' She opened the doors and folded them back so they could see.

'Blimey,' breathed Bugsy.

After that, nobody spoke for long seconds, then Jack pulled on a pair of the latex gloves that he always kept in his pocket for such occasions and climbed up into the van. He got as close to the body as he dared without disturbing anything around it — and without upsetting Doctor Hardacre by contaminating her crime scene. He touched an arm briefly, then climbed out. 'He's stiff as a board. Rigor is well set in.'

'Well, it would be, wouldn't it?' declared Corrie. 'The body's been there since I got back last night. Thanks to the cold weather, it hasn't attracted flies, yet. Do you think you could get someone to take it away without anyone seeing?'

'No, Corrie, of course I can't. You know the drill. This place will have to be cordoned off and uniform will keep people out until Dr Hardacre and SOCOs have done their examination. We may have to close Coriander's Cuisine altogether.'

She gasped. 'Jack . . . no! We're right in the middle of our busiest time. I've got a ton of orders, all over Christmas and into the New Year. You can't close us down.'

'Do you recognize the deceased, Mrs D?' asked Bugsy. 'Course, I realize you can't see his face properly — it's covered in some sort of yellow slime.'

'I beg your pardon!' Corrie protested. 'That "yellow slime" is what remains of a peach Bellini trifle. It's one of my superior desserts for seasonal dinner parties and a delicious and lighter alternative to Christmas pudding. And no, I don't recognize him.'

'Ah. Sorry, Mrs D.'

'Did you find any ID, Corrie?' asked Jack, hopefully.

She shuddered. 'No, I didn't. I haven't dared touch him.' She saw Jack's face fall. 'It's all very well for you, you're used to finding dead bodies all over the place. Look at it from my point of view — some malicious person steals my best vegetable knife, stabs some random victim, then dumps the body in my van. If I didn't know better, I'd think it was someone with a grudge, trying to put me out of business.'

'That's a bit extreme, sweetheart,' said Jack. 'I'm assuming you haven't fed anyone dodgy prawns or a poisonous mushroom recently?'

'How very dare you! My food is of the utmost quality, prepared from the finest ingredients. What irks me is that I didn't know he was there until I got here this morning. I keep thinking if only I'd opened the van doors while it was in Eden Park and I was messing about trying to get it started, the crime scene would have been deemed to be there, instead of in the garage outside my business.'

Bugsy muttered to Jack. 'If he hasn't actually been inside the kitchens, guv, maybe we can limit the cordon to the garage and the car park. Then we wouldn't need to close Mrs D down.'

Jack's brow was furrowed which meant he was thinking hard. 'Our corpse might have been hiding in the van when the killer climbed in, grabbed your knife and stabbed him.' He glared at her. 'Corrie, I can't believe you left the van unlocked while it was unattended. How many times have I talked to you about security? Apart from knives that cost more than my last month's salary, you've got a lot of expensive kit in there — mobile ovens, hot-holding equipment, that sort of stuff.'

She protested. 'Normally I do lock it, but this was Eden Park, Jack — a safe, gated community. It's bristling with security guards, CCTV, self-appointed neighbourhood busybodies peering through their designer blinds, and rich residents with vicious watchdogs and state-of-the-art burglar alarms.'

'Which means on a dark night around Christmas, when folk are out at company parties and business dinners, or sunning themselves in the Caribbean with their vicious watchdogs in kennels, it's probably bristling with burglars, too.'

She bridled. 'Well, how was I to know someone would take the opportunity to shove a corpse into my van?'

'If he was killed somewhere else,' mused Bugsy, 'I reckon it would take more than one person to heave him inside.'

'But if he was killed somewhere else, how would they have got hold of one of Corrie's knives?' Jack reckoned they were speculating — Bugsy reckoned they were pissing in the wind. Either way, what they really needed was a proper crime scene investigation and answers from the experts. 'Bugsy, rustle up Big Ron and her body snatchers, and I'll get Norman to send over his uniform lads . . . and lasses,' he added, as a hasty afterthought. Gemma, the team feminist, would be proud of him.

* * *

At that precise moment, Gemma and her colleague, Aled, were interviewing Darren, the young man who helped with the milking on Bert Cook's dairy farm. When the constable showed him into the interview room, it was clear from his body language that he had a deep-seated dislike of law enforcement in general and the police in particular.

Gemma began. 'How long have you been milking cows for Mr Cook, Darren?'

He leaned his chair back and balanced it precariously on two legs. 'No comment, and I don't fink you're allowed to question me wivout a solicitor. And you ain't cautioned me, neither.' He'd been through the procedures a few times in his young life and thought he knew how it was supposed to work.

'We don't need to because you're not under arrest,' Aled assured him. 'You're just helping us with our enquiries. We just want to know a bit about the farm.'

'You'd better ask Mr Cook, then.'

'We have,' said Gemma. 'Now we're asking you. How long have you been working on the farm?'

'Since my last stretch inside. 'Bout eighteen months ago. And before you start stirring it, trying to get me sacked, Mr Cook did know I'd been in prison when he gave me the job.'

'Do you help with anything else?'

'Nope. Just the cows.'

'What about feeding them?' Aled was trying to find out how much Darren knew about silage.

'Fred does all that.'

Aled knew that Fred was the other farm worker who was full time and had been with Cook for ten years. He'd never been in any trouble with the police, but that didn't mean he wasn't capable of murder. If you listened to Velma, thought Aled, she reckoned most people don't believe they're capable of murder until it happens. It just needs the right kind of provocation under the right circumstances.

'What do you know about silage, Darren?' probed Gemma.

'Nuffink, except it stinks. Sort of sickly, like. Why?'

'When does Fred start feeding it? What time of year?'

He looked baffled. 'I dunno. When there's no grass left, I s'pose. What's silage got to do wiv anything? I thought this was about some dead tart that old Bert found this morning. I came in to start the milking and the place was crawling wiv coppers.'

'Do you know anything about that, Darren?' asked Aled. 'Did you know the dead girl? What was her name?'

He thought about this for a bit, then the light dawned. 'Oh no you don't!' He stood up and pushed his chair away. 'You ain't pinnin' nuffink on me. I know you lot. You're lookin' for a result — don't matter who the poor bugger is as long as you get a conviction. Just because I've got form, you reckon I'm an easy collar. Well, you're wrong. I don't know nuffink about no dead girl and if I'm not under arrest, I'm getting' out of here.' He made for the door. Aled nodded and the uniformed constable opened it for him and followed him out.

After he'd gone, Aled looked across at Gemma. 'I don't think we made a very good job of that, do you?'

'To be fair, he was hostile when he came in. As soon as he thought we were going to fit him up, he was never going to cooperate.'

'Do you fancy him for it?' asked Aled. 'He's the right age to have been involved with the deceased. Big Ron reckoned she was between eighteen and twenty. Maybe she was his girlfriend. They had a row and he strangled her. Mind you, I doubt if he could have shifted the tyres and tarpaulin, heaved her body up on the silage, then covered it all back up on his own. He didn't have the muscles for it. Apart from which, the report says there were two sets of footprints. What d'you reckon?'

Gemma shook her head. 'No. I don't fancy him for it. He showed no kind of emotion when he mentioned her. Not passion, anger or jealousy, just total indifference. "Some dead tart". He's either very smart or very thick — my money's on the latter.'

* * *

When Doctor Hardacre arrived at Corrie's catering facility, Jack had instructed uniform to cordon off just the garage and part of the car park as the crime scene. He agreed with Bugsy that since the deceased had remained in the back of Corrie's van throughout, with the van and garage doors locked, it could be argued that the kitchens were not places of interest in the investigation.

The pathologist donned the customary protective suit and greeted Jack with her usual gusto. 'Well, here we are again, Inspector. Two bodies with scarcely three hours between them. Must be a record, even for you. If you're going for a hat trick, let me know and I'll hire more mortuary attendants.'

She climbed into the van. After a long preliminary inspection, making notes by talking into her recorder, she called to the scene-of-crime officers. 'Can we turn him over, please? Carefully — there's an embedded weapon and samples will need to be taken.' When three of the SOCOs stepped forward, she stopped them. 'No, just one of you, please. There isn't much room for manoeuvre in here.'

As they turned him over, Bugsy peered inside. 'Looks like he may have been beaten up, guv. I can see blood on his face.'

'That isn't blood. It's raspberry compote from my peach Bellini trifle,' hissed Corrie, between gritted teeth.

Finally, having carefully gathered anything that might be described as forensic evidence, Doctor Hardacre gave permission for the body to be removed from Corrie's van, placed in a body bag and loaded into a mortuary vehicle. As they zipped up the bag, Corrie caught sight of the dead man's face. It was only the merest glimpse, but it was enough. She gulped and turned away.

'You all right, Mrs D?' asked Bugsy. 'You've gone very pale.'

'Yes, you have sweetheart,' agreed Jack. 'You've had a very nasty shock. I think you should go home. Your ladies are quite capable of carrying on without you. You can catch up with them tomorrow.'

Corrie took a deep breath so her voice didn't shake. 'Yes, I think I will go home. I'll see you later, Jack.'

It was at this point in a murder investigation that Jack, as SIO, would interview whoever found the body. He doubted there was much more that Corrie could tell him but decided that he would talk to her tonight, over supper, after she'd had a chance to rest.

* * *

Corrie drove very carefully, conscious that her reaction time might not be as snappy as usual. When she got home, she made a mug of tea, took it upstairs and ran a hot bath. As she lay back in the scented bubbles, she tried to get the whole ghastly situation straight in her mind before she decided what her next move should be. She was sure, now, that the body in her van was Tom's. It seemed like a lifetime since she last saw him, but the receding chin, the wart on his nose and the domed forehead hadn't changed much over the years. She still had his note written on a *Corrie's Kitchen* napkin in her handbag.

She wondered how much she should tell Jack — if anything. Tom had obviously fallen foul of some seriously dangerous people. She recalled his message: *"Andie, I'm in trouble. I need somewhere to hide. Please help me for old times' sake."* Well, she hadn't had the option to help him, had she? He'd been murdered before she got the chance.

They'd both been ridiculously young when they married — barely twenty. A flashback of their ill-fated honeymoon returned with ghastly clarity. Would she ever forget it? She had spent the whole turbulent two weeks in a bathroom in Provence with food poisoning. It had been a traumatizing experience but was probably one of the motivations behind her decision to forge a career in catering. In any event, it wasn't a good start to the marriage and a year later, Tom left her for Eva, a robust Scandinavian fitness instructor. The last she'd heard, they had moved to Sweden and opened a fitness centre with saunas, cold plunge pools and bunches of those twiggy things that you beat yourself with. When she'd given him any thought at all, which was hardly ever, she'd believed he was still there and happily married — until today.

A sudden thought made her blood run cold, despite the warmth of the bath. When the police eventually identified Tom, and she was sure they would with all the methods at their disposal — DNA, fingerprints and all that tricksy, scientific malarkey that can match you to an eyelash — Clive, the team's digital forensic specialist, would delve into Tom's past. Clive was a master delver. If there was a delving event at the Olympic Games, Clive would win gold. It would take him no time at all to find out that the deceased had once been married to the woman in whose van his body had been found — skewered with her Japanese Santoku knife. She sat bolt upright causing a bow wave of bath water to cascade over the side and across the floor. The stark reality of her situation kicked in. Things had taken a very nasty turn.

CHAPTER FIVE

At two o'clock precisely, Doctor Hardacre performed the post-mortem on the young woman's body found on the silage mound. She was a stickler for timekeeping and solicitous about her charges, even though they were beyond harm. She hadn't wanted to keep this one lying about in the mortuary any longer than was necessary. The examination confirmed what she had already suspected — the cause of death was manual strangulation and had occurred during a four-hour window between ten at night and two next morning. She could find no evidence of alcohol, drugs, vaping or cigarettes, not even caffeine, which some pathologists might consider unusual in a modern young person, but she believed she had a good idea why this young woman hadn't wanted to pollute her system with poisons. She and Marigold Catwater exchanged glances.

When Jack and Bugsy arrived, she gave them the standard information — height, weight, toxicology and stomach contents.

'She ate her last meal less than an hour before she died. Chicken and salad. It was still in her stomach, virtually undigested.' She picked up a stainless-steel dish. 'Would you like to see?'

39

'No thanks, Doctor. I'll take your word for it,' Jack replied hastily. He hated the morbid atmosphere of the cold, white-slabbed mortuary room. The disinfectant smells always stuck in his throat and made him queasy. He feared that looking at someone's stomach contents in a dish might cause him to contaminate them with some of his own.

'No tattoos, scars or birth marks to help with identification, I'm afraid, and the killer was careful to remove any piercings or jewellery she might have been wearing. There's an indentation on the third finger of her left hand which indicates a recent engagement ring or even a slim wedding band.' She lifted the small, white hand so Jack could see.

'So, that means there's probably a partner kicking around somewhere,' deduced Bugsy. 'Why hasn't he or she reported her missing?'

Doctor Hardacre continued. 'There's evidence that the deceased tried to fight off her killer. She had acrylic nails of the kind done professionally in a nail salon. They're very striking — red and green with a silver star on the tip. Some of them are broken. Miss Catwater will send you pictures. The edges are sharp so your killer may have some scratches. I found a microscopic amount of tissue under one of them. I've sent it off to be tested, but unless the killer is on the system already, it won't help very much. At least, not until you have a suspect. Then we can try a match.'

'We're following several lines of enquiry, Doctor, but we're some way off finding a suspect. No record of the young woman's prints or DNA on the database, I suppose?'

'No, sorry. You might find this useful, though. She's had some very expensive work done on her teeth recently. Veneers, whitening — that kind of thing. And she had blonde extensions in her hair. It's quite an expensive process as I understand it. Marigold will send you images of those, too.'

Bugsy tried to imagine Big Ron with blonde hair extensions and couldn't. She had dark, very short hair and a moustache to match, and he had to concede, a scientific brain that was second to none.

'I'll get the team to do a trawl of nail bars, cosmetic dentists and hairdressers, see if that turns up anything.' Jack looked down at the slim, shapely figure lying on the autopsy table. 'She was very beautiful. Such a terrible waste of a young life.'

'It's a waste of more than just one life,' revealed the pathologist. 'This young woman was pregnant, Inspector. About eight to ten weeks, I'd say.'

'That's very sad,' said Jack.

'Would she have known, Doc?' asked Bugsy.

'Almost certainly. A good-quality test kit can detect a pregnancy in as little as five days after conception. It explains why I could find nothing in her system that would have been toxic to a developing embryo. For whatever reason, she wanted to keep this baby safe and healthy.'

Jack frowned. 'So, that means that whoever strangled her has committed two murders.'

'Make sure you catch him, Jack.' Doctor Hardacre hardly ever called the inspector by his first name but she was more than usually affected by this murder.

'We will, Doctor. Thanks.'

They turned to leave but she called after them. 'Don't forget the post-mortem on the dead man we extracted from your wife's van, Inspector.' She made him sound like a bad tooth. 'Shall we say eight o'clock tomorrow morning?'

'Fine. We'll be there.'

* * *

Using the information Doctor Hardacre had emailed through from the post-mortem examination, Aled updated the white-board which had now become a storyboard. Anyone on the team could add information to it, but he kept it relevant and coherent. He had drawn a line down the middle with a photograph at the top of each column, separating the two cases. In the absence of any identities, he labelled them "Silage Lady" and "Van Man". Although it might be construed as a little

41

insensitive, it did make clear which information belonged to which victim, although the details under "Van Man" were, as yet, sparse. Apart from the deaths having apparently occurred within hours of each other, there was nothing to connect them. And the locations of the bodies couldn't have been more disparate — under the silage tarpaulin on a farm in Richington Cross and in the back of a catering delivery van on the outskirts of Kings Richington. But like the boss had said, murders can be like buses, none for ages then two come along together. That didn't mean they were linked.

Bugsy looked at the photo of the dead girl. He shook his head in disbelief. 'What sort of bloke throttles a pregnant woman? I don't understand and I never shall.'

'Maybe the "bloke" in question didn't know she was pregnant, Sarge,' suggested Gemma.

'And maybe it wouldn't have made any difference if he had,' added Velma.

'I don't think we should assume that her killer was the person whose ring she was once wearing.' Gemma never jumped to obvious conclusions. 'It could have been her dad, an uncle or some random who broke into her bedroom, strangled her and stole her jewellery.'

'Or even, given that she was wearing glamorous pyjamas, some rough antics in bed that went too far.' Aled wasn't speaking from personal experience, but he did spend a lot of time on Netflix.

Bugsy still looked puzzled. 'Come on, DC Dinkley, we have to catch this bastard. Give us a profile.' He corrected himself. 'I mean, give us your conclusions about the probable behaviours and psychology of our killer.'

Velma had informed him that the term 'profiler' was not formally used in UK law enforcement, but whatever the job title, it served the same purpose. She considered the facts for several moments then began. 'Some partners, mainly men, can act very irrationally in response to an unplanned pregnancy, especially if they suspect, rightly or wrongly, that they may not be the father.'

'Well, I reckon that's understandable,' declared Aled. 'It questions a bloke's manhood.'

She ignored him, having neither the time nor the inclination to discuss the causes of some men's fragile notions of their virility. 'Considering the frenzied behaviour of our killer and the evidence provided by the forensics teams, the statistical probabilities indicate that this young woman was, in fact, killed by her partner but that someone else did the "tidying up". They removed any obvious means of identification and found somewhere to put the body where they believed it wouldn't be discovered for a long time. Our killer would have been too enraged and out of control to think for himself about the practicalities of covering his tracks, so I think somebody else did it for him.'

'But why would anyone do that?' questioned Aled. 'According to the laws of joint enterprise, if you're seen to be involved in the commission of a murder, you could be seen as equally guilty as the person who committed it. You'd have to be barmy to even think about it.'

'It's either someone who cares enough about our killer to want to protect him . . .' suggested Velma.

'. . . or someone who was paid a lot of money to do the clearing up,' finished Gemma.

'This is all very interesting,' said Jack, 'but our first priority is to find out who she is and notify her relatives.'

'Who still haven't reported her missing,' Clive pointed out.

Gemma began emailing all the nail bars in the area with photographs of the broken acrylics to see if anyone remembered creating that design recently. Clive was trawling cosmetic dentists with details of the deceased's teeth veneers and Velma was trying her luck with the hairdressers. Time-consuming, tedious work but that's what murder investigations were all about.

It was while they were busy on the telephones that Fred Lynch turned up on the front desk. Bert Cook had told him that the police wanted to speak to him so he thought he'd get it over with. One of Norman's constables showed him into an interview room and Gemma and Aled paused their enquiries to go down and take his statement.

'Thanks for coming in, Mr Lynch,' Gemma began. 'We appreciate that your work on the farm has been disrupted enough as it is.'

Fred coughed nervously and fidgeted in the hard chair. 'That's right. Poor old Bert — I mean, Mr Cook — still hasn't got over the shock. I've never seen him so upset. He said you needed to speak to me about my part in all this. I don't know what I can tell you. I wasn't there when he found that young woman's body. I was as shocked as anyone. Bert didn't reckon on feeding that silage for a long time yet. She could have stayed there undisturbed for months — years even.'

'You've worked for Mr Cook,' Aled consulted his notes, 'for over ten years. Is that right?'

'Yes. He's a good boss and I like to think I'm a good worker.'

'Can you think of any reason why someone would hide a body on his farm in particular?'

'No, I can't. I said to Jean, my wife, "What's the world coming to? A strange young woman turns up dead, wearing just her nightclothes and an old blanket, and with all her jewellery missing." What kind of folk can do that to another human being?'

'We found two sets of boot prints in the silage of the kind you're wearing now. We believe they belonged to whoever carried her up there.' Gemma was chancing her arm and watched him for some kind of reaction. Not a flicker, although she was sure he was nervous. But she conceded that many people were anxious at just being in a police interview room, without being guilty of anything.

He pointed to his boots. 'We all wear these — me, Bert, and the lad, Darren. They're standard footwear for tramping about the farm, especially in the snow. You can buy them online. I expect that's how the criminals got them.'

The interview continued with the usual background information, and half an hour later, Fred Lynch signed his statement and Aled showed him out.

Back in the incident room, Gemma was pensive. 'I wonder how Lynch knew that the body was wearing nightclothes and wrapped in an old blanket if he wasn't there when Cook found her.'

'I daresay Cook told him,' replied Jack. 'They probably talked about it. It's what some people do when they're stressed — they talk a lot.'

'What motive could he possibly have for killing a young woman half his age?' wondered Bugsy.

'Maybe it was him who put her in the club,' said Aled. 'He's got a wife and two kids. Maybe she threatened to tell them.'

'If anyone put her in the club, my money would be on Darren Fletcher, although I don't think he killed her,' declared Gemma. 'He's a chippy little sod. He'd be more likely to regard pregnancy as proof that his balls work than a motive for murder.'

* * *

When Jack got home that evening, he could tell Corrie was still upset because she was cooking — on an industrial scale. When she was stressed, she cooked. It was her way of restoring her equilibrium. Other people did yoga, meditation, walked the dog or ate a giant chocolate bar. Corrie cooked. There were regiments of tarts, pies, pastries and cakes, some chilling out on racks and many more queueing up, waiting for their turn in the oven.

'Hello, sweetheart.' He picked up a warm doughnut and bit into it. 'How are you feeling?'

'I'm OK, thanks. Just catching up on some orders.' She ducked. 'Don't you dare kiss me with sugary jam on your lips.'

Jack decided that his best approach was to act normally, to give her the chance to talk about the elephant in the room, or rather the body in the van, in her own time. At some point, they had to take a statement from her as the person who found the body, but he had no intention of doing a formal SIO's interview on his own wife. He wasn't even sure it was allowed. He would ask Bugsy to do it.

Corrie carried on egg-washing the puff pastry on a batch of mince pies. She knew she owed it to Jack to explain that she'd recognized the dead man, but she wasn't sure she wanted to do it yet. It would add another dimension to the already difficult situation she was in and, by association, implicate Jack too. Bad enough, she thought, to find a corpse killed with a knife that you knew would have your fingerprints on it, but for the body to turn out to be your ex-husband was really pushing your luck. She supposed she was nursing a forlorn hope that the murder investigation might go ahead without her connection to Tom ever being discovered. It was, after all, a long time ago. On the other hand, she realized the note he wrote to her, still in her handbag, was integral to the case and a possible clue to the killers he was running from. She should offer it as evidence. In the end, after much soul-searching, she decided she would wait to see what the post-mortem — and Clive — turned up. She started on another battalion of mince pies.

* * *

It was looking very jolly in the Richington Arms. The landlord had gone to a lot of trouble to pull in the punters over the Christmas period so he could sell copious quantities of alcohol and food to justify the expense. Lights on a large Christmas tree flashed on and off in the corner and a roaring log fire crackled in the grate. He'd strung twinkly lanterns around the bar and along the window frames and nailed bunches of plastic holly and mistletoe to the imitation oak beams. Customers were even given a cheap cracker with every bar meal. They were rejects he'd bought from the market and only one in every ten had a snap in it, but he felt they added to the festive vibes.

Despite the cheerful atmosphere, Joe sat in the corner on his own, looking glum and sipping his pint. He met Tom there most nights. Neither had any family to speak of and they each lived alone in scruffy bedsits. They had drifted into some kind of mutually morose companionship to watch football on the big TV or discuss the terrible cost of beer and, inevitably, the cold weather. It was better than drinking alone. Joe knew what Tom did to scrape a living. It wasn't that he approved of breaking into folk's homes and nicking their stuff, but a bloke had to do something to earn a crust. As for his own occupation, he worked as a bouncer at The Tempest Club. His proper title was "door supervisor" but when you analysed his job description, he was employed to either chuck people out or stop them from coming in. He knew all sorts of crooked dealings went on there. Blokes were frogmarched into the back room for a "meeting" with Bernie Shakespeare and frequently hobbled out covered in blood and minus a few teeth. Large quantities of drugs changed hands, no questions asked.

Joe minded his own business and took his pay at the end of the week. It was safer that way. But when he'd got wind of the birthday party being planned for the boss, and tables that had been booked for the whole family, it meant the big, posh mansion in Eden Park would be empty until late into the night. It seemed like a golden opportunity for Tom with rich pickings. He'd tipped him off in return for a share of the loot. They were going to divvy up the spoils tonight, but Tom hadn't turned up. It wasn't like him. Of course, he could have just pushed off with all of it. Burglars weren't renowned for their honesty. Joe wondered if he should report him missing if he didn't appear by the end of the week. He doubted that anybody else would. But given the nature of Tom's occupation, Joe thought it probably better to stay clear of the cops.

CHAPTER SIX

It was eight o'clock on a bitterly cold morning and Jack had slept badly the previous night, conscious of Corrie tossing and turning beside him. They hadn't spoken much as work beckoned for them both but he knew she had something on her mind and she would tell him in her own good time.

Doctor Hardacre's examination room felt as cold and cloying as ever. He and Bugsy trooped in, nodded to Miss Catwater and stood to one side of the autopsy table.

'Good morning, Inspector Dawes, Sergeant Malone. Good to see you both again, but we must stop meeting like this — people will talk.' That was as close as Big Ron got to light banter. Gallows humour might be Sergeant Malone's way of dealing with harrowing situations, but it wasn't hers. She pulled back the sheet covering the man's body and went through the basics as she had done with the young woman the previous afternoon, although the lifestyle of this individual had been very different.

'This man is between forty-five and fifty-five, underweight, poorly nourished with evidence of a long history of chest infections. I found evidence of alcohol and smoking but not to excess. He broke his tibia and fibula sometime in the past — at a guess, I'd say he had a fall. Cause of death

— a stab wound in the back that severed his spinal cord, and penetrated a lung and a main artery. He would have died very soon after.' She pointed to the knife enclosed in a sterile bag. 'The weapon is a Japanese knife, very sharp, mostly used by chefs — only one set of fingerprints, no match on the database.'

'They'll be Corrie's,' said Jack. 'The killer must have worn gloves. Can you give us time of death, Doctor?'

The doctor was hesitant. 'I'd say around eight hours before Mrs Dawes found him. Estimating time of death is still one of the least reliable processes. There are just too many variables that can skew results for it to be an exact science. But forensically, there's something about this body and where it was found that doesn't add up. It's the lividity.'

'I'd be livid, too, if someone stuck a knife in my back,' quipped Bugsy.

She gave him a scathing look and continued, undeterred. 'Post-mortem lividity, gentlemen, is the process where blood pools in dependent tissues following cessation of the circulation. It stains the skin a purplish colour and it's visible in almost all bodies . . .' she paused for emphasis '. . . except those that have undergone a massive haemorrhage. Lividity here was minimal because a wound like this would have caused huge blood loss — but I found very little blood in the van.'

'Wouldn't leaving the knife in the wound help to stem the blood flow, Doc?' asked Bugsy. He was no expert but felt sure he'd read it somewhere.

'Yes, partly, Sergeant. It might go some way to explaining the lack of blood in the van but it doesn't explain the lack of lividity in the body. In my opinion, this man had bled out.'

'So, where did all the blood go?' asked Jack.

'Fathoming that out, Inspector Dawes, is a job for a detective. Miss Catwater will take fingerprint and DNA samples and send copies to your office. Good day, gentlemen.'

* * *

Back in the incident room, Gemma, Clive and Velma had spent most of the day phoning round the nail bars, dentists and hairdressers in an attempt to identify the young woman with the broken acrylics, expensive veneers and hair extensions. The room was filled with the chatter of one-sided conversations. It had been a long and tedious exercise.

When Jack returned, he called out to the team, 'Do we have a name for silage lady, yet?'

'Venetia Adler!' said Gemma.

'Venetia Adler!' agreed Clive.

'Venetia Adler!' confirmed Velma.

'There's a guy who owns a nail bar in Richington called Funky Tips, explained Gemma. 'He remembers doing a set of acrylic nails like the ones I emailed him. He remembered it particularly because the client wanted something Christmassy so he designed red and green nails with a silver star on the tip. She said it was her favourite time of year apart from Hogmanay.'

'Pity the poor girl won't get to see it,' muttered Bugsy.

'I've just spoken to a private cosmetic dentist in the city,' reported Clive. 'He recognized his work when I emailed him the pictures of her teeth. He said he'd be happy to confirm it formally from his records if required.'

'Venetia Adler had her extensions done regularly at a salon in town. They recognized her photograph,' added Velma.

'Right,' said Jack. 'It's pretty certain our silage lady is Venetia Adler, then. Well done, team. Do we have an address? We need to get in touch with her relatives, get a formal identification.'

'The address she gave the dentist is a house in Eden Park,' said Clive.

'That's that compound in the snobby part of Kings Richington,' said Aled.

Gemma scolded him. 'It isn't a compound, Aled. You make it sound like they're in prison.'

'Some of 'em ought to be, if you ask me. Either that or a zoo. Have you seen the gorillas patrolling the gates?'

'Aled, you shouldn't use "gorilla" as shorthand for aggressive, dominant male behaviour,' Gemma admonished. 'It's anthropomorphism implying they can act without regard to the rights of others and the law.' She lowered her voice. 'And anyway, I've seen those blokes and I think I prefer gorillas.'

Clive was tapping away on his computer. 'According to the Eden Park Private Residents' Association, the house belongs to Bernard Shakespeare. He's lived there with his wife and two sons for over fifteen years. The house and grounds are reckoned to be worth upwards of two million.'

'How do you get into those kinds of records?' asked Aled, impressed.

'Clive can hack into anything,' said Gemma.

'Blimey,' breathed Bugsy. 'You know who Bernie Shakespeare is, don't you, guv?'

'Indeed I do.' Jack frowned. 'I imagine every law enforcement agency in the land knows who The Bard is. The Met and the NCA have been after him for years, but nothing ever seems to stick. He's always one step ahead. Probably because he has lots of friends in high places. He runs a very resourceful organization.'

'That's because witnesses are too scared to give evidence against him,' said Bugsy. 'There was that one bloke they put in witness protection. You remember him, guv — little bloke, pencil moustache, horn-rimmed spectacles, wore a wig. He reckoned he saw Bernie take a cut-throat razor to one of his gang rivals in a club in Soho and was prepared to testify. The Protected Persons Service gave this little bloke a new identity, new wig, new glasses and a new location, miles away. They even shaved off his moustache, just to be on the safe side. Absolutely untraceable, they said. He'd be perfectly safe until it was time for him to give evidence. They found him the following week in Bridlington, nailed to his own front door.'

Aled grimaced. 'That's terrible. No wonder nobody wants to go to court.'

'Even if they actually lived long enough to give evidence, Bernie would manage to wriggle out of it,' commented Jack. 'His personal barrister is Sir Gregory Munro, KC.'

'I've heard of him,' recalled Gemma. When she was studying law, she had toyed with the idea of becoming a barrister. 'He's reckoned to be the best in the business — and the most expensive.'

'And corruptible, by the sound of it,' added Aled.

'Here it is — Eden Park,' announced Clive, who hadn't been listening. He was looking at Shakespeare's house on Google Earth. 'Wasn't that the area where Mrs Dawes was delivering food and Van Man turned up in her trifle the next day?'

Jack had already made the connection in his head. He was still sure there was something she wasn't telling him. *Dear God, Corrie. What have you got yourself mixed up in this time?* His fears were interrupted by Clive's next announcement.

'Speaking of Van Man, sir, I've traced his fingerprints and DNA on the police database. His name's Tom Broadbent and he'd built up quite a record.'

Bugsy was looking over his shoulder. 'Blimey. He's been pinched more times than a barmaid's bottom.'

Gemma's eyebrows shot up into her fringe. One of her crusades, and she had many, was to reverse negative female stereotypes. 'I don't think you're allowed to say that, Sarge. Not these days.'

Bugsy bowed theatrically. 'Humble apologies, DC Fox. Have I inadvertently fallen foul of another of your "isms"? I've just about learned to avoid racism, ageism and sexism and now I know to steer clear of anthropomorphism but I hadn't realized there was a barmaid-ism. It's just a figure of speech. No offence to barmaids intended. All the same, this bloke's been in and out of Brixton nick like it had a revolving door.'

Clive scrolled down. 'He had numerous convictions for breaking and entering, theft and burglary for which, as the Sarge says, he served several terms in a Class C prison. He obviously wasn't very good at his job. On one occasion, he was arrested trying to escape from Boots after he'd dashed in and grabbed fifty quid's worth of toothpaste. A police constable nicked him with his arms full of boxes, struggling to push open the door when the sign on it said "pull".'

'What else do we know about him, Clive?' Jack feared there was more to come and hoped there might be something to explain, convincingly and innocently, why he ended up dead in Corrie's van.

'He seems to have made good use of his time in prison — technology classes, fitness training, electronics . . .'

'All skills to make him a better burglar,' observed Jack, grimly.

'He was future-proofing his career, sir,' suggested Aled.

Clive continued scrolling through Broadbent's files. 'His medical records say he broke his leg when he fell off a roof trying to pinch a satellite dish. And he suffered from rhotacism.'

'Flippin' heck, not another "ism",' muttered Bugsy. 'What do I have to be careful of this time?'

Clive explained. 'You mustn't ridicule someone who has problems with his "r's".'

'I shouldn't dream of it,' protested Bugsy. 'It could be haemorrhoids, flatulence, threadworms — any number of unpleasant conditions. I've suffered from a few myself.'

'No, Sarge,' Clive said, keeping a straight face. 'Rhotacism is the name they give to a speech disorder. It's the defective pronunciation of the letter "r".'

Bugsy snorted. 'Are you telling me that's the best they could come up with? The word to describe the inability to pronounce "r" is a word beginning with "r"?'

'Yep. That's about it, Sarge.'

'So, the poor devil couldn't even tell you what was wrong with him. Unbelievable.'

'Clive, can you find anything on his files about his earlier life? Before he decided to become a burglar?' Jack thought it might help.

Clive tapped and scrolled for several minutes. 'He lived in Stockholm for a few years, running a fitness centre with a woman named Eva Larsson. There was some problem with the accounts, money going missing, tax evasion. Eventually, the business was transferred to her name and the Swedish authorities deported him back to the UK. Before that, in his early twenties, he was married to . . . erm . . .' He read it several times to make sure he wasn't mistaken. It couldn't be right, could it? If it was, reading it out loud was well beyond his pay grade. 'Sarge, could you come and look at this, please?' Bugsy went across and peered at Clive's screen. They were both silent for some minutes.

'Well?' Jack was impatient. 'What have you found?'

'It's a copy of a marriage certificate, guv.' Bugsy chose his words carefully. 'Of course, it would need checking out. It might not mean anything at all. It was a long time ago. It's probably just a coincidence.'

'Spit it out, Sergeant. Who did he marry?' asked Jack, fearing he already knew the answer. 'Was her name Coriander?'

'Yes, Jack,' Bugsy was concerned. 'But that doesn't prove anything. There must be lots of women with the same name.'

The room went very quiet. The team realized this was not the time to ask questions or make assumptions. They waited for DI Dawes to tell them what they should do next.

He looked at his watch. 'It's been a long day. I suggest we have an early finish and start again tomorrow morning. Thanks for all your hard work, team.' He strode out.

* * *

Driving home, Jack was mulling over the two murders in his mind. There was no connection — or so he had thought. But now there was a tenuous link. Eden Park. Venetia Adler had lived there, in Bernie Shakespeare's millionaire mansion, and Tom Broadbent had been killed there, allegedly in Corrie's parked van. Now there was more than an even chance that Corrie and Broadbent had once been man and wife. He'd always known that Corrie had been married before but she never spoke about it and neither had he. It was a long time ago and had not been a good experience for her. He feared that now he'd have to ask her a few questions because if he didn't, somebody else would — probably Chief Superintendent Garwood. He wondered how best to broach the subject when he got home. He didn't have to.

* * *

Corrie could tell from Jack's face that Clive had delved, as she had feared. He'd discovered Tom's identity and that she had once been his wife. She had been expecting it. Apart from feeling foolish, she felt relieved.

'Jack . . .' she began, 'I was going to tell you, but . . .'

He put his arms around her. 'You recognized him, didn't you?'

'Yes. I didn't know what to do. That note on the napkin — it was from Tom. He gave it to Carlene — I knew it was from him, but I honestly didn't expect him to turn up dead in my van.'

'Of course you didn't, sweetheart. Have you still got it?'

'Yes. It's in my handbag.' She fetched it and handed it over.

Jack read it. 'He called you "Andie".'

'Yes because . . .'

'He couldn't pronounce "Corrie". Yes, I know.' He read the note again. 'He obviously knew his life was in danger but they got to him before he could escape.'

Corrie frowned. 'Who's "they"? Are you allowed to tell me?'

'Probably not, and anyway, I don't know for sure. But I have a strong suspicion a gangster named Bernie Shakespeare is at the back of this. I don't know how or why. but I'm going to find out. There are too many coincidences and I don't believe in coincidences.'

'So, what happens now?'

'Nothing's changed. I still have two murders to solve.'

But things had changed, radically, as Jack discovered when he got to the station the next day.

* * *

When Jack arrived in the incident room, there was an urgent summons waiting for him. Chief Superintendent Garwood wanted to see him in his office as soon as he got in.

George Garwood cared about the efficiency and clear-up rate of his team only inasmuch as it reflected on his chances of promotion and his hopes of retiring as Commissioner and with a knighthood. He was generally regarded as pompous, pedantic and paranoid about getting on the wrong side of anyone that mattered. Paradoxically, this frequently caused him to make ill-advised decisions that worked against him. The editor of the *Richington Echo* regularly took a swipe at him whenever he felt the police were dragging their heels. Garwood could never understand how the press got information faster than he did.

He suspected that more went on in the incident room than he knew, because Dawes and his team were selective about what they told him. This time, thanks to Ethel, the tea lady, he was one step ahead of them. When she wasn't working in the police canteen, Ethel did a stint peeling vegetables in the kitchens of Coriander's Cuisine. She'd been there when the mortuary men in white coats had taken away a body from Mrs Dawes' delivery van.

Jack tapped on his door.

'Come!' Garwood sat behind his highly polished mahogany desk, pens and pencils lined up alongside his blotter, perfectly parallel and exactly five millimetres apart. His computer was set to one side and barely used, which accounted, in part, for his lack of up-to-date intelligence. Emails were lined up in serried ranks, unopened and unread. While not best practice, it enabled him to say, "I'm sorry, sir, I didn't get that email," when questioned by the commander on an important issue that he knew nothing about.

Jack pushed open the door and strode in. 'Sir. You wanted to see me?'

'Yes, Inspector.' Garwood gestured towards a man sitting on the other side of his desk. 'This is DI Crump from Q Division. He will be taking over as Senior Investigating Officer on the Broadbent case.'

Opposite him sat a plump, unremarkable man in a badly creased suit that was too small for him. He was balding with odd wisps of ginger hair, eyebrows that met in the middle and ears too large for his head. Small round spectacles, held together with a piece of fuse wire, sat halfway down his nose. The long end of his tie, which bore witness to the egg he'd had for breakfast, was tucked into the waistband of his trousers while the short end poked out just below his shirt collar.

Crump stood up to shake hands. His trousers shot up a good six inches shy of his shoes, due to a pair of perilously overstretched braces. He beamed, amiably. 'Pleased to meet you, Inspector Dawes.'

Jack was bewildered. 'But I thought . . .'

'Yes, I expect you did,' interrupted Garwood, 'but you can't possibly investigate a murder in which your wife is the main suspect.' He stood up, steepled his fingers and walked up and down his office, pontificating. 'You must know that a police officer can have no part in any investigation in which he is, in any way, personally involved. Such a conflict of interest could be used by a barrister to manipulate the outcome of a trial.'

'But, sir . . .' Jack was caught on the back foot. He hadn't seen this coming although, with hindsight, he realized he should have.

'Ethical firewalls, Inspector,' boomed Garwood. He had come to a halt in front of the window from where he could see his new car, neatly parked in the space bearing his name. In his imagination, the sign morphed into "*Sir* George Garwood". He smiled.

'Pardon, sir?' asked Jack.

Garwood returned to the present. 'I see no reason why you shouldn't continue to head up the investigation into the murder of the young woman, Venetia Adler. As far as I can see, Mrs Dawes is not a suspect and the cases are not connected in any way. But you must observe a strict firewall, gentlemen. There must be no sharing of information that might lead to ethical or legal violations. Is that clear?'

'Yes, sir,' they chorused.

'That will be all. Carry on.' Garwood waved them away. After they'd gone, Garwood rubbed his hands together, gleefully. That showed Dawes that he was on the ball. The Inspector had an uncanny way of making him feel inadequate. Nothing he could put his finger on, no insubordination or anything specific that he could slap down. Just an air of intellectual superiority which irritated Garwood immensely. His wife, Cynthia, said it was because he secretly believed that Jack *was* intellectually superior, which was rubbish. He went across to the drinks cabinet and poured himself a generous whisky to celebrate. This time, he was ahead of the game.

CHAPTER SEVEN

In the lift up to the incident room, Dawes was still reeling. Crump was humming to himself. Jack hadn't expected Garwood to bring in another DI to deal with the death of Corrie's ex-husband. And what did he mean — she was the main suspect? He wasn't aware that Garwood knew anything about it. He never took an interest in any case until it was successfully resolved and he could take all the credit. Jack braced himself. He should introduce Crump to the team. It was only courtesy as he was going to be leading them on the Broadbent case.

'How do you want to handle this, DI Crump?' Jack asked.

'Please, call me Percy.' He smiled, vacantly. 'I've no idea. I thought you might have a few suggestions. What was all that stuff about a firewall?'

'It's a virtual barrier erected to block the exchange of information between teams. DCS Garwood says we mustn't share any intelligence because it could compromise a conviction.'

Crump shrugged. 'Well, that's going to make things a bit difficult, isn't it? How are we supposed to know what the other one's doing if we don't share information?'

Jack took a deep breath. 'I believe that's the idea, Percy.'

'Well, I think that's daft.' He was silent for a few moments. 'Did your wife really knife her ex? You can tell me, Jack.'

'No, she definitely did not, Percy.'

'Pity. It might have hurried things up a bit. The Hammers are playing Arsenal next Saturday and I was hoping to be back by then.'

They'd reached the fifth floor and the doors opened. There was a bit of polite 'after you' — 'no, after you', until eventually they both squeezed through, side by side. Jack wondered if this was an omen.

The team had been waiting impatiently to find out what was going on. Bugsy reckoned if the old man wanted to see the DI urgently, something brown and smelly was about to hit the fan and Garwood wanted to deflect it in Jack's direction. When Dawes and Crump came in, the room went quiet.

Jack walked to the front with Percy. 'This is DI Crump. He will be investigating the Tom Broadbent murder. I want you to give him all the support you can.' *He's going to need it*, thought Jack. 'I shall continue to work with some of you on the Venetia Adler case. We have been told we must operate behind firewalls because of the involvement of Mrs Dawes in one of the cases and a possible conflict of interest.'

There were jeers and shouts of 'Rubbish, sir!' and 'Don't believe it, sir'.

Jack held up a placatory hand. 'Thank you for your support. I really appreciate it, but all the same, I think we must be seen to keep the cases separate. Aled, can you arrange two whiteboards, please, one at each end of the room? And electronic communications must be shared only with the appropriate officers.' That was as far as Jack was prepared to go with a firewall. Where Corrie was concerned, he had every intention of keeping a close eye on everything Crump did. From what he'd seen of him so far, Crump was quite capable of arresting and charging her simply because she was his only suspect and West Ham were playing Arsenal on Saturday.

* * *

The Shakespeares' luxury home in Eden Park had a spacious orangery where Bernie and Teresa liked to take coffee and croissants in the morning, read the papers and admire the snow scene that covered their stylish garden. Enclosed with evergreen hedging for privacy and with key plants strategically placed to catch the low light of the winter sun, it had been designed by a grateful landscape architect whose much older and much richer wife had "disappeared", courtesy of Bernie's hit-squad, leaving him a great deal of money.

That morning's copy of the *Richington Echo* had just been delivered. The headline screamed *Dead body found in the delivery van of local caterer, Coriander Dawes. Murdered man identified as ex-husband, Tom Broadbent.* The following article described the kitchen knife that had been used to stab him and stated that it had belonged to Corrie Dawes, owner of Coriander's Cuisine, a successful catering company.

Bernie Shakespeare was incandescent and Marco had been summoned to explain the debacle. 'Haven't I taught you anything?' Bernie seethed. 'What have I always told you? Get rid of the body and don't leave anything that could be traced back to you or the firm. The Shakespeare syndicate has a reputation of always cleaning up its own mess — never leaving anything behind for the cops to find.'

'But Papà, there wasn't time to plan anything. The guy was lying there, bleeding into the snow. Then I spotted this old green van parked down the road. The doors were unlocked so me and the boys picked up the body and we slung it in the back. It was full of cooking stuff — pots and pans and food scraps. I reckoned that when they found him with a kitchen knife in his back, the cops would reckon whoever owned the van had "offed" the guy.'

What enraged Bernie most was that Marco was grinning as if he was actually proud of his ingenuity, rather than showing contrition for having committed one almighty cock-up. The tirade continued. 'Why didn't you chuck him in the river? Under a train. In the back of a bin lorry. Anywhere that would make it difficult to identify the body. The police have pathologists, clever scientific people who can find the smallest piece of evidence. Haven't I always told you that killing someone is the easy part. Getting rid of the body is when you have to be clever. And if you smirk at me again, boy, I'll knock your head off!'

Teresa jumped up, seized Marco, and clasped his head to her bosom. 'No, you won't!' she shrieked at Bernie. 'Leave him alone. He did his best. He remembered to wear gloves, didn't he? What more do you want? How did the papers get hold of it, anyway?'

* * *

That was what Jack wanted to know. Corrie was devastated. They both knew that nobody on Jack's team at the station would have revealed sensitive information to the press — apart from their loyalty, it would have cost them their jobs. It had to be someone else. But who else knew?

'Jack, this could ruin my business,' fretted Corrie. 'It'll put a lot of people out of work.'

He tried to comfort her. 'You've had worse press, sweetheart. What about the time you catered Cynthia Garwood's posh bun-fight and everyone went down with food poisoning?'

'That was nothing to do with my food, Jack. Someone spiked Cynthia's jam with anti-freeze. It was all explained at the trial and I was exonerated. And anyway, that's not the same as being exposed as a murder suspect. If I find out who leaked the information to the *Echo*, I won't be responsible for my actions. Can't you lean on the editor and make him tell you?'

''Fraid not. Journalistic material's protected from police seizure under PACE. I'd have to make an application to a judge and I doubt if they'd rule that the informant should be named just so you can punch his lights out. When I get back to the nick, I'll make a few enquiries. It could take a while.'

In the event, it didn't take any time at all. When Jack had settled at what they were now calling the "Pavilion End" of the long, sloping incident room, DI Crump trotted up from the "Nursery End", beaming.

'Morning, Jack. What did you think of my piece in the local rag? Good, eh? I'm hoping there'll be something on the TV news, too.'

Jack swallowed hard. 'Percy, are you telling me that it was you who leaked the information about my wife to the press?'

'That's right. You'd be surprised what crawls out of the woodwork once you make a case public and ask for information. We did it all the time at my last nick. Saves a lot of leg work.'

Jack couldn't believe his ears. Neither could the team who were listening avidly. 'Did it never occur to you what damage that kind of publicity can do to an innocent party?'

'Your wife, you mean? Ah, but we don't know she's innocent yet, do we? I've sent a car for her. Thought I'd bring her in for a little chat. 'Course, you can't be involved, can you?' He tapped his nose with his forefinger. 'Firewalls and all that.' He toddled back down to his end of the room.

Bugsy appeared at Jack's side bearing a mug of strong coffee. 'Calm down, guv. You're going a funny colour.'

'You know what they say, sir,' added Gemma, proffering a chocolate digestive from her secret hoard. 'Don't get mad — get even.'

'That's right, sir,' agreed Aled. 'We're going to crack the Broadbent case as well as the Adler murder. That'll show him. Bugger the firewall. I'm keeping a close eye on DI Crump's whiteboard.'

'And I've set up a covert intranet system so that I can tap into his messages,' said Clive.

Velma chewed her lip, a sure sign that she was psycho-analysing something. 'I'm testing the hypothesis that any link between Eden Park and our two murders is purely coinciden-tal. Statistically, it's highly unlikely.'

Although Jack was grateful and touched by the loyalty of his team, he didn't want them getting into trouble on his account. 'That's really helpful, guys, but be careful. If the Chief Super finds out, we'll all be for it.'

* * *

Joe sat in his usual seat by the fire in the festive Richington Arms, but he wasn't feeling very merry. He was reading a piece written by the editor of the *Echo* about the body that had been found in the back of a delivery van. There was a picture. Only head and shoulders, but it was him all right. Poor old Tom. At least they'd spelled his name right. Tom hadn't double-crossed him and made off with the loot after all. They must have caught him at it. Stabbed, it said. If anyone had any information, they were to come forward and speak to the police. Not bloody likely, thought Joe. It wouldn't help Tom. Not now. Joe had been on the door of The Tempest Club, the night of Bernie's birthday party. It had been rammed and as far as he could tell, all the Shakespeare family had been there, drinking champagne and eating cake. The tip-off had been a good one. The house should have been empty.

He hadn't realized that Tom had once been married. He'd never spoken about it. There was a picture of her, too. Coriander Dawes, owner of a catering company, Coriander's Cuisine. From the way it was written, it looked like the police thought she might have done it. Joe knew better. Bernie Shakespeare was at the back of this — he'd put money on it if he had any. At the same time, it seemed a bit extreme even for Bernie. If he'd caught Tom breaking in, he might have ordered his men to give him a good kicking, break a few bones, but stabbing him in the back wasn't his style. Neither was shoving the body in the back of someone's van. Bernie had more permanent ways of getting rid of people. Joe reckoned there must have been more to it than that.

* * *

When the police car pulled up outside Coriander's Cuisine, Joyce, the supervisor, assumed it would be someone from the station to speak to Corrie. Everyone had seen the body being taken from her van and the subsequent revelations in the press naming the murdered man as her ex-husband. It was the most excitement they'd had for ages.

They all gawped, surreptitiously, as Constable Johnson unwound his six-foot-six frame from the passenger seat and walked towards the unit. He took off his hat, brushed off the snow and pushed open the door. He was met by appetizing aromas of spices, dried fruit and brandy that reminded him of his nan's kitchen at Christmas. This is a good place to work, he decided, especially in this weather.

'Is Mrs Dawes here, madam?' he asked Joyce.

'Yes, she's in the office, down the corridor.' She pointed.

Constable Johnson tapped on the door and went in. Corrie recognized him from when she had catered Ladies' Night at the Richington Golf Club. Uniform had been called to break up an affray and he had sustained an injury to his ear from a flying five-iron. She had applied sage oil to it.

'Hello, Constable Johnson. What can I do for you? Mince pies, Christmas cake, a Yule log for the holiday season? It'll save your mum or your wife having to cook.'

'No thanks, Mrs Dawes.' He looked embarrassed. 'I've been instructed to accompany you to the station for an interview.'

'Oh. Right. I'll get my coat.' Corrie wondered why Jack hadn't come himself or asked her what he wanted to know at home. It must be something that had to be seen to be done officially.

PC Johnson escorted her to the car, opened the back door and guided her head in.

'Has Mrs Dawes been arrested,' asked one of the young pastry cooks.

'No, of course not. Don't be silly.' But Joyce wasn't as convinced as she sounded.

* * *

It was a twenty-minute drive to the station during which neither the driver nor PC Johnson spoke, which Corrie thought was odd. When they arrived, he led her to an interview room on the ground floor and opened the door. A short, chubby man was seated on the far side of the table. He stood up when Corrie came in. At five-feet-one, he was just one inch taller than her.

'Mrs Dawes. Please sit down. I'm DI Crump and I'm investigating the murder of Tom Broadbent.'

'Oh. But I thought my husband . . .'

'Yes, I expect you did, but DI Dawes is no longer handling this case. We're operating behind firewalls.'

'Excuse me?' Corrie hadn't realized how confused you can become when you're sitting opposite a police officer with a big, thick notepad and an urgent ballpoint. She was fascinated by the food stains on his tie and was trying to work out what they had been in a previous existence. She decided on baked beans and ketchup.

DI Crump was droning on about the need to ensure he had all the necessary details and background information. He asked her about the time she had arrived at Eden Park on the night in question, how long she'd spent on each of the deliveries and the names and addresses of the customers. He wrote it all down in laborious longhand. Corrie fumed inwardly. She'd given all this information to Jack before he disappeared behind a firewall. For goodness sake! Why didn't the man use a digital recorder?

Percy looked at what he'd written, scribbled out some of it, then tore off a page and screwed it up. 'Did you see anybody else hanging around when you got back to your van — apart from your ex-husband?'

Corrie took a deep breath. 'Mr Crump, I have already explained several times, I hadn't seen my ex-husband in over twenty years until I opened the doors of my van the following morning and found him lying in the back. Even then, I only recognized him after the pathologist turned him over and I saw his face. Have I made myself clear this time?'

'So, what you're saying is that there weren't any witnesses to the murder?'

'There may have been. I wasn't there when the murder took place, so I wouldn't know, would I?'

'But he was stabbed with your own chef's knife — the knife that you say was in your van and has never left your possession — so you must have seen someone . . . unless . . .' He stood up and leaned forward to emphasize his point, but his braces twanged alarmingly so he sat down again. '. . . unless you did it yourself. Shall I tell you what I think happened?'

If you must, thought Corrie.

'Tom Broadbent turned up out of the blue, probably asking for money. We know he didn't have any, which is why he'd done time for stealing. When you saw him, all the old acrimony came back. All the bitterness and jealousy. He left you for another woman. I'm guessing a younger, more attractive woman.'

Thanks for that! Probably true though. Corrie had no illusions.

'You snapped, grabbed the knife from the van and when he turned his back on you, you stabbed him. That's what happened, isn't it?'

'What about CCTV?' asked Corrie, hoping to steer him back to evidence instead of guesswork. 'There are loads of cameras in Eden Park. Have you looked at the film?'

He coughed. 'Erm . . . they don't seem to have been working. Some sort of fault on the line.'

She ran out of patience. 'I'm sorry, DI Crump, I'm not entirely sure why I'm here or why we're doing this. Are you going to charge me? Do I need a solicitor?'

'No, no. It's quite all right, Mrs Dawes. Nothing to worry about — not yet anyway. Just one more question. Where did you go after you stuck the knife in your ex-husband?'

CHAPTER EIGHT

On the Dawes side of the firewall, Jack's team was attempting to construct a timeline of Broadbent's last movements, despite it no longer being their case. Clive had obtained the CCTV footage that showed him running from Bernie Shakespeare's house, pursued by the Eden Park security guards. They watched it, anxious to pick up the smallest detail that might help. The cameras stopped recording at the perimeter gates.

'We've lost him,' said Aled. 'Where did he go between here and when he ended up in the back of Mrs Dawes' van?'

Jack filled them in about the visit to the takeaway and the napkin on which Broadbent had written the note to Corrie. 'Incidentally, I haven't shared this information with DI Crump.' Jack tapped the side of his nose. 'Firewalls.'

'I'm not sure the note helps us, sir.' DC "Chippy" Chippendale was a bright officer, newly recruited to MIT and desperate to find a clue in the hopes of becoming one of DI Dawes' inner circle of detectives. 'DI Crump could argue that after Broadbent found out about Coriander's Cuisine and had written the note, he ran into Mrs Dawes doing her deliveries and recognized her. She realized who he was and offered to let him hide in her van. Then she stuck a knife in him.'

'Why?' asked Bugsy. 'What's your motive?'

Chippy shrugged. 'I don't know, Sarge. Because he'd deserted her for another woman? Hell hath no fury and all that?'

'But Mrs Dawes isn't the kind of woman to bear a grudge, not after all these years,' said Gemma. 'She did what any woman with balls would do — she got on with her life.'

'For the sake of argument, Chippy, let's say you're right. Why would she take the body back to her catering unit and lock it in the garage?' Jack was impressed by the young copper's thinking.

'What else would she do with it, sir? She needed time to decide the best way forward.'

'So, she calls the station and reports it?' Bugsy was doubtful. 'No, I don't think that stacks up, son. Doc Hardacre reckons Broadbent bled out, so where did all the blood go? And anyway, the working hypothesis is that she didn't do it.'

'I'm confused,' said Aled. 'Bear with me, everyone. As I understand it, Broadbent breaks into Shakespeare's house in Eden Park to see what he can nick. He's only a petty thief, but even so, we must assume he knew who the house belonged to, so he was taking a huge risk. Something panics him and he sets off the alarms so he has to leg it. He disappears out of range of the CCTV, then twenty-minutes later, he turns up on the CCTV of a takeaway in Kings Richington and goes inside for a burger. Mrs Dawes' last delivery was to an old bloke in Eden Park and it was while she was in his house that we reckon the body was put in her van that she'd left parked down the road. So, having got away from Eden Park alive, why did Broadbent end up back there — and dead?'

'Aled has a point, sir,' said Clive. 'There are whole chunks of Eden Park CCTV footage missing. 'I've got Mrs Dawes going into Maurice Blake's house with his meal, then there's a gap until she's back at her van, scraping the windscreen. Someone has cut and spliced the footage. It's been cleverly done but it's quite obvious if you know what to look for.'

'And during that gap, Broadbent was knifed and stashed in the van.'

Jack frowned, concentrating. 'Who has charge of the CCTV cameras in Eden Park?'

'The security guards, sir,' replied Clive. 'And they're all paid by—'

'Bernie Shakespeare,' finished Jack. 'Just as I thought.'

'One thing puzzles me, guv,' said Bugsy. 'Broadbent didn't get away with anything in the end. When we saw him running, he wasn't carrying a ninety-inch telly under his arm, was he? So, why would Shakespeare have him topped?'

'I suppose he could have had a couple of Rolexes in his pocket,' said Velma, 'but it's more likely, as Voltaire said, he was killed *pour encourager les autres*. On the other hand, it might have been for another reason entirely, unrelated to the burglary.' She had that distant expression that told the others she was exploring an altogether different possibility.

'Bearing in mind that the murder case we are supposed to be working on is that of Venetia Adler,' said Jack, 'I think it's time we visited the Shakespeare household to find out how long she'd lived there and why nobody has reported her missing. Clive, do we have anything else on this young lady? Her parents, siblings, anything like that?'

'No, sir. Nothing I can find on any of the national databases or any of the private ones. I'm not even sure that Venetia Adler was her real name.'

Jack reached for his coat. 'Carry on digging, Clive. Sergeant Malone, you're with me.'

* * *

Engraved on the ornate plaque above the front door of Bernie Shakespeare's mansion in Eden Park was "New Place". Bernie had named it after William Shakespeare's house in Stratford-upon-Avon, bought in 1597 after he had amassed sufficient wealth to afford a new family home. Bernie identified with this and considered it apt, although he doubted that the real Shakespeare had made his money the same way he had.

Bernie's mansion also boasted a swimming pool, tennis court and gym. It was unlikely that Will had had those, either.

Jack stopped in front of the wrought-iron electric gates and held up his warrant card to the camera. He spoke his name into the intercom then threaded the car through the double gates as they slowly yawned open. He followed the tree-lined drive until it culminated in a circular courtyard at the front of the house. In the centre was an ostentatious, three-tier fountain with a carved granite surround. Marble dolphins frolicked around a naked nymph holding aloft a giant shell from which water cascaded down into the fish-pond below.

Two burly gardeners were trimming the long hedges without much enthusiasm. Bugsy guessed, rightly, that they were bodyguards rather than horticulturists. One of them approached the car. He had a deep scar down one cheek and a cauliflower ear. 'Can I help you, gents?'

'DI Dawes and DS Malone to see Mr Shakespeare.'

The man glanced briefly at the warrant card. 'There's nobody home except Mrs Shakespeare. You'll have to come back another time.'

'That's OK,' said Jack, getting out. 'We'll speak to her.'

For a moment, Bugsy thought the man was going to grab Jack's arm and he braced himself for a scuffle, but the fellow obviously had second thoughts and escorted them to the door.

Teresa Shakespeare saw them coming on one of the many video cameras that were installed around the house. She had learned during her marriage to Bernie to be prepared for such visits, both from the police and rival mobsters. She dealt with it while keeping up the pretence of respectability that was so important to his business.

'Mrs Shakespeare?' asked Bugsy, pleasantly. 'I'm DS Malone and this is DI Dawes.' They held out the warrant cards again. 'Can we have a word, please?'

'What's it about?'

'A young lady by the name of Venetia Adler.'

Jack noticed the brief flicker of recognition before it disappeared. 'My husband and sons are at the club. You should speak to them.' She went to close the door, but Bugsy put his foot in it.

'We shall, madam, but in the meantime, could we have a few words with you, now that we're here?'

'You have warrant?' She knew the drill.

'No, Mrs Shakespeare,' said Jack. 'We don't want to search your house, just have a brief chat.'

She stood back, reluctantly, thinking that cooperation would attract less attention than confrontation. 'You better come in.' The Sicilian accent was distinctive but not unattractive. Her glossy, black hair was tied up into a loose bun and she wore a pale lemon, cashmere trouser suit with a silk scarf. Bugsy reckoned she must be on the wrong side of fifty-five. His wife, Iris, would have described her as well preserved.

The drawing room was full of what Jack considered clutter, but expensive clutter — large ceramic animal sculptures, ugly paintings by disturbed artists and a stuffed leopard crouching in the corner, baring its teeth ready to pounce. It was the kind of decor owned by someone with a great deal of money who wanted to appear cultured but obviously wasn't.

'Please sit down.' Teresa Shakespeare didn't offer them any refreshment. She wanted the police out of her house as soon as possible so she wasn't about to delay their departure by making them tea. 'What is it you want to know, officers?'

'According to our records, this young lady lived here.' Bugsy whipped out a photo of the dead woman and handed it to her — tactics designed to shock the recipient into dropping their guard. Not in this case. This woman had seen too much violent crime during her lifetime to be easily shocked.

Teresa looked at the photo for what she considered an acceptable length of time then handed it back. 'Yes, I recognize her. She lived here for a while.'

'Did she work for you?' enquired Jack.

'No.'

Jack probed. 'She didn't work here, but she lived with you. Why was that?'

'She was engaged to my son, Marco.'

'When did you last see her?' Bugsy sensed the lioness protecting her cub.

Teresa sniffed. 'I can't remember. She came and went as she pleased. This is a big house with many rooms. I haven't seen her for some time.'

No love lost there, thought Jack. It explained why Venetia hadn't been reported missing. He suspected that the CCTV on the gate wouldn't be any help in tracing her movements. It would show exactly what Bernie wanted it to show. 'Would it surprise you to know that her body has been found? She's been strangled.'

Teresa showed no emotion. 'No, it wouldn't surprise me at all, Inspector. She was . . . *buttana* . . . slut. I was glad when Marco ended their relationship. She wasn't right for him. Always half-naked in skimpy clothes, too much makeup — and all that blonde hair and fancy fingernails. Girls like that come to a bad end.'

Bugsy reckoned if DC Fox had been there, she would have given the woman a lecture about stereotypes. He'd already decided that the customary "sorry for your loss" speech would be a bad idea. 'Do you have any thoughts about who might have killed her, Mrs Shakespeare?'

She shrugged. 'It could have been any of the men she flirted with. The slut got what was coming to her.'

'How long was your son engaged to her?' asked Jack.

'He wasn't . . . not properly.' She brushed it off. 'It was just a stupid mistake that he regretted. The little tart was just after his money and she thought that once she'd got her claws in . . .'

'Do you think we could take a look around her room?' asked Bugsy.

'No! Not without a warrant. I don't want the police snooping around my house without a good reason.'

'We'll need someone to identify the young lady's body,' said Jack. 'Would your son be able to do that?'

'No. Find somebody else. There must be lots of men who are more than familiar with that whore's body.' She stood up. 'Now, if you've finished, Inspector, there are things I need to do.'

They trooped to the front door and just as they were leaving, Bugsy did his ingenuous double-take. 'Just one more thing, madam. According to the post-mortem report, Venetia Adler was pregnant. Was your son, Marco, the father?'

This time she really did lose her composure. 'No! No! How dare you even suggest it! Go away!' She slammed the door.

They could hear her still screaming Sicilian obscenities as they sauntered back to the car.

'I think it would be safe to say Mrs Shakespeare didn't know,' said Jack.

Bugsy nodded. 'More to the point, did Marco know? Do you want me to get a warrant so we can search her room?'

'No point. By the time we get in there, Mrs Shakespeare will have had it stripped of everything, right back to the wallpaper.'

* * *

Teresa watched the two police officers climb into their car and drive away, then she grabbed her phone and punched in Bernie's number. He was in the Tempest Club discussing business with Grant.

'What with the increased cost of living and the price of energy that it takes to run our clubs efficiently these days, the cost of protection on all the businesses we control has to be increased . . . say, by ten per cent. Make sure the boys know that when they do the monthly collections and report to me if anybody objects or refuses to pay.'

'Yes, boss.' Grant was his enforcer-in-chief and kept the others in line. He was roughly the same age as his son, Jonnie, and Bernie relied on him totally to sort out all the routine stuff. Grant went off to pass on the order.

Bernie saw Teresa's number come up on his phone and pressed connect. He could hear her having hysterics, mostly in Sicilian.

'Teresa, what's the matter? What's happened?'

'It's all your fault!' she shrieked. 'You promised me they wouldn't find her body for months, maybe even years. Well, they have found it and the police have been here, asking questions.'

'Calm down. What did you tell them?'

'What do you think I told them? What do I ever tell the police? Nothing! I told them nothing.' She gulped, then spat out the words. 'Bernie, that little whore was pregnant.'

Bernie's face was grim. 'I wonder if Marco knew.'

Teresa started shrieking again. 'Marco wasn't the father! I don't believe it. It could have been anyone — she slept with many men. It wasn't Marco!'

'For goodness sake, Teresa. You don't know that. You're making accusations because you didn't like her — because she was beautiful and sexy and your precious Marco was besotted with her.'

'He didn't love her! Not really. He would never have married her. Never! I'd have killed her myself before I'd let that happen.' She tried to think clearly. 'What are we going to do?' she demanded.

'Nothing.' Bernie was thinking fast. 'We do nothing. I just need to tie up a few loose ends. Pour yourself a brandy and take a couple of pills.' He ended the call then went to find Grant.

* * *

'Grant, remember that little job I asked you to do, the night of my birthday party?'

'Yes, boss. What about it?'

'It seems to have gone badly wrong. The police have . . .' he searched for suitable words, '. . . discovered the problem.'

Grant was shaken. 'They can't have. The guy said he knew a place where the problem wouldn't be found for a very long time. That's why I used him.'

'Well, he was wrong. Did this guy help you with the job?'

'Yes, boss, in return for wiping his slate clean at the casino. He was into us for a big wedge.'

Bernie studied his fingernails thoughtfully, then polished them on the lapel of his immaculate RAF blazer. He'd never been anywhere near the armed forces, but he thought the badge lent him an air of integrity. 'I don't think we can trust him to keep quiet, do you? He could cause us a lot of grief. I need you to make sure that he doesn't.'

'Yes, boss. Leave it to me. I'll see to it.' Grant left, wondering if he'd ever be promoted to a position in the syndicate where he'd get to do something other than the dirty jobs.

* * *

Jack and Corrie had both had long days. Corrie was too worn-out to cook supper, having spent several tedious hours at the station, being interrogated by DI Crump. Jack still had Teresa Shakespeare's shrieks of protest ringing in his ears without having obtained anything useful. They decided to eat out and were sitting upstairs in Chez Carlene, soothed by its ambience and the accordion music playing softly in the background. The Michelin-starred bistro, in the trendy food and drink quarter of Kings Richington, had a strong French influence and was very popular. It had become the favourite rendezvous of busy professionals wanting to iron out the kinks after a stressful day.

'How did you get on with DI Crump?' asked Jack.

Corrie rolled her eyes. 'He kept asking me the same inane questions. Why did I stab Tom? Had we been seeing each other behind your back? Was he blackmailing me? What had I intended to do with his body? Honestly, Jack, he's convinced I did it and he isn't even considering the possibility that it might have been someone else. He let me go today, but I'm sure it's only a matter of time before he arrests me.'

Jack dipped a piece of bread in aioli sauce. 'Sweetheart, he can't charge you. He doesn't have any evidence.'

'He thinks he does. He said only my fingerprints are on the knife and on the doors of the van.'

'Circumstantial.' Jack pierced an olive with a stick.

'It's all right for you, skulking behind your firewall,' protested Corrie. 'What are you doing to find Tom's killer before Crump throws me in the slammer?'

'Don't worry. The team is working hard to solve both cases — Broadbent and Venetia. Velma is convinced they're connected.'

'Velma . . . is she the brainy one in a baggy sweater and square horn-rimmed spectacles?'

'That's her. She has this theory that Tom's body in your van and the last address of Venetia both being in Eden Park is not a coincidence. Apparently, Big Ron's report that they were killed within hours of each other, plus a whole lot of other complicated psychological analyses, mean that according to the laws of probability and statistics — it was the same killer.'

'That can't be right, surely? What possible motive would a murderer have for killing both Venetia Adler, the beautiful fiancée of the heir to a criminal empire and failed burglar, Tom Broadbent?'

'I agree. In the vast sewer of criminal behaviour, Broadbent was a bottom feeder. Sorry, darling.'

'No, you're right. Even years ago, when we first got together, I remember that he didn't have much of a work ethic. I suspect that's why he was chucked out of the fitness centre in Sweden.'

Carlene, who worked front of house in her bistro, had been visiting each table to ensure that diners were happy and had now reached Jack and Corrie. 'Hello, you two!' She kissed them both on the cheek. 'Have you ordered? The *escargots de Bourgogne* are particularly good.'

'No, not snails, thanks.' Corrie recalled that snails had been the reason she'd been confined to the bathroom during her entire two-week honeymoon with Tom. She'd discovered that they moved considerably faster after you'd eaten them than they did when they were alive.

Carlene sat down at the table and lowered her voice. 'Mrs D, are you OK?' Although she hadn't said so at the time, she'd read the note that the weird bloke had written on the napkin before she'd given it to Corrie. She thought it meant trouble and she'd been right. Then the press revealed that the man had actually been Corrie's ex-husband. Until then, Carlene hadn't even been aware that Corrie had an ex-husband. She'd never talked about him. 'Mrs Garwood was in at lunchtime and she said you'd been arrested.'

'Not yet,' said Corrie, 'but I think I might be, very soon.'

Carlene turned on Jack. 'Inspector Jack, can't you do anything about this?'

'No, he can't,' retorted Corrie. 'He's hiding behind a firewall.'

'In that case,' she whispered in Corrie's ear, 'this is a job for the three C's. I'll ring you.'

CHAPTER NINE

'I think it's time we had a little holiday,' Fred Lynch announced to his wife, Jean. He'd come home early from the farm, telling Bert he was going to take some time off because he had quite a lot of leave owing. What he didn't tell him was that he wouldn't be coming back. The fewer people who knew it, the better.

'That would be lovely, but can we afford it?' They were always short of money and Jean knew why. Fred gambled most of his pay before she saw a penny of it. People said it was an addiction, but she reckoned, in Fred's case, that was just an excuse. He just enjoyed gambling away their money. It certainly wasn't the prospect of winning that attracted him because he lost far more than he ever won.

'Yes, of course we can afford it, love. I've had a nice little win down the club,' he lied. 'We'll take the kids and go somewhere warm for Christmas.'

'How long will we be gone?' she asked. 'I need to know what to pack and the kids will be off school for the Christmas holidays soon. If we're gone longer than that, the school will have to be informed.'

Fred was impatient and snapped. 'I don't know how long we'll be gone, but we have to leave tomorrow!'

'Why so soon?' Jean sensed trouble.

'Because I say so, that's why! Don't argue!'

The children were excited. 'But what about Santa? How will he know where to bring our presents?'

'We'll leave him a forwarding address,' promised Jean.

That's exactly what we won't do, thought Fred, grimly. As soon as he'd heard that Bert had uncovered the silage and found the girl's body, he'd known that he needed to get the family away — somewhere they wouldn't be found. He'd given his statement to the police, like they asked, but it wasn't them he was afraid of. He wished he'd never got involved, but he was into the casino at the Tempest Club for thousands. Grant, Bernie Shakespeare's lackey, knew he worked on a farm and when he'd offered to clear the debt in return for helping him get rid of a body, it seemed like the perfect solution. He had assured Grant that the body wouldn't be found for months, possibly years. How was he to know that Bert would bring in the cows and uncover the silage much earlier than expected? But it didn't do to cross Bernie Shakespeare, everyone knew that.

Fred stayed up most of the night working out the travel arrangements. He'd drive them to Dover and take the ferry to Calais. It was the quickest route. They'd be in France in about an hour and a half. Once they were out of the country, they should be safe. He didn't think Bernie's empire stretched too far into Europe but you never knew. They would travel south and into Spain. He didn't have any money, but Jean had some savings stashed away in a biscuit tin that she thought he didn't know about. He'd take the money from there. He didn't dare tell her what he'd done. She'd never understand that he'd been desperate.

Early next morning, before it was light, they loaded up the car. The kids were hyper, chattering and stuffing favourite toys and snacks into their backpacks. Jean was anxious — this wasn't just a "little holiday" was it? She didn't know why they had to leave in such a hurry and without telling anyone, but she wasn't daft. She sensed it was something bad, but she didn't want to know the details.

'Fred, why can't I tell Mum and Dad where we're going? They'll worry if they come round and nobody's home.'

'You can ring them from France. Come on! We need to leave now if we're going to catch the ferry.'

Finally, they were all in the car and the house was locked. Fred reckoned he'd post the keys back to the council once they were safe. His in-laws would take care of their belongings. He started the engine, turned on the headlights and was about to reverse out of the drive when Jean put a hand on his arm.

'Fred, I've left our passports on the kitchen table.'

'Jean, for Christ's sake!' He jumped out and dashed back to the house, sweating despite the freezing temperature. He unlocked the front door, grabbed the passports from the kitchen and hurried back out. Jean saw him reappear on the front step, lock the door again then turn towards the car. For a split second, he was caught in the full beam of its headlights. There was a bang, like a small sonic boom. It put up a flock of starlings, roosting in the nearby trees. From the passenger seat, Jean watched, horrified, as a small hole burned into Fred's forehead, right between his eyes. He slid slowly down the front door until he was sitting on the step, staring straight ahead. She screamed and screamed.

* * *

'Sir, we've got another one. Fred Lynch out at Richington Barrow. Shot dead on his own doorstep.' Aled had taken the call. 'Uniform reckon it looks more like an execution than murder.'

'Blimey, that's three,' said Bugsy. 'Big Ron will think we're doing this on purpose, just to keep her off the streets.'

'But we only interviewed Lynch a couple of days ago,' said Gemma. 'He just came in, volunteered general information about the farm and how long he'd worked there, and signed a statement. Nothing contentious that was likely to get him shot.'

Jack was sombre. 'What did you make of him, Aled?'

Aled thought about it. 'Not a lot, really, sir. He seemed nervous, but who wouldn't with DC Fox on their case? Enough to put the wind up anyone. Ouch!'

Gemma had grabbed his ruler and clouted him with it. 'Lynch went to great pains to tell us that he hadn't been there when Mr Cook found Venetia Adler's body yet he knew what she was wearing and that her jewellery had been removed.'

'Like you said, guv, Cook might have discussed it with him, but I doubt it,' offered Bugsy. 'Old Bert was genuinely traumatized. I don't think he'd have wanted to talk about it any longer than he had to.'

'Clive, anything of interest in Lynch's financial history?' asked Jack.

'Only that as soon as he got paid and the money was in the bank, he drew out large sums in cash every week. Might have been housekeeping for his wife.'

'Or money to spend on drink or gambling that couldn't be traced back to him,' suggested Gemma.

'OK, Bugsy, let's get out there and have a look around,' said Jack. 'Gemma, Aled, you too. I'll need you to speak to the widow, do a door-to-door and get a family liaison officer arranged. I understand there are children. Velma, Clive, in the meantime, can you get a fix on what's happening with DI Crump and Mrs Dawes, please? Ring me if there's anything you think I should know.'

* * *

A forensics tent stood in the front garden of Lynch's house and police tape secured the area. Constable Johnson, blue with cold, stood on guard. He'd been there since just after dawn when the call came through. He acknowledged Jack and nodded towards the tent. 'Morning, Inspector. Doctor Hardacre is already inside. There are relatives in the house, looking after Mrs Lynch. I believe they're her parents.'

'Thanks, Constable. Gemma, do you want to go in and see what the police can do to assist? Aled, I can see lights going on in the neighbourhood. Can you knock on a few doors and ask if anyone saw or heard anything useful?'

The pathologist emerged from the tent when she heard Jack's voice. 'Morning, Inspector. It's bloody cold in there and these polyethylene suits don't help. No confusion about the cause and time of death, though. Bullet through the brain a couple of hours ago.'

'Can you tell what type of firearm it was, Doc?' asked Bugsy.

She pursed her lips. 'You'll need to speak to a ballistics expert for a forensic analysis, but at a guess, I'd say something powerful and accurate at long range. This is the work of a sniper, and a good one.' She pointed to the block of apartments across the road. 'From the angle it entered his skull, I'd say it came from that top flat. But like I say, ballistics branch are the experts at identifying trajectory. I'll give them the bullet.'

'I suppose you'll have to dig it out of the poor bugger's head at the post-mortem.' Bugsy pulled a face.

'No need, Sergeant.' She held out a dish. 'It went right through his head and into the front door. Miss Catwater dug it out.'

Jean Lynch's parents took their grandchildren into another room while Gemma spoke to their mother. She was very shocked and Gemma wondered if she should call an ambulance.

'No, I don't need an ambulance. My mum will look after us.' Jean sipped the tea Gemma had made and the cup rattled in the saucer when she put it down.

'Are you OK to answer a few questions, Mrs Lynch? I know it sounds insensitive, but it's always better to ask them as soon as possible after the . . . er . . . event, while it's still fresh in your mind.'

Jean took a long, shuddering breath. 'It's certainly fresh in my mind, officer. I don't think it will ever go away. We were sitting in the car, the kids and me, waiting for Fred to come back with the passports. He came out the front door, turned around and there was this loud bang. It made the kids jump. And Fred just dropped . . .' She blew her nose into a tissue.

'Where were you going?' asked Gemma. 'It must have been a very early start.'

'Fred was taking us on a little holiday to France over Christmas. The kids were so excited.'

'Had you been planning it for a while?' Gemma wondered.

'No. Fred only suggested it last night. He said he had some holiday owing and he'd had a win at the casino.'

The mention of a casino alerted Gemma to a possible connection to Bernie Shakespeare's clubs. They were where all the main casinos in the area were located. Fred Lynch hadn't come across as a compulsive gambler, but Gemma knew they came in all shapes and sizes and were good at concealing it. And it would explain the large sums of cash that Clive had said Lynch drew out every week. 'Did Mr Lynch have any enemies?'

'No, absolutely not. He was a good man, a hard worker, and everybody liked him. It must have been a terrible accident or a mistaken identity.'

It never ceased to amaze Gemma that after someone died, all their faults miraculously disappeared and posthumously, they became wonderful blameless human beings. This sanctification made it extremely difficult to identify anyone with a motive for their murder.

'It was all my fault,' sobbed Jean. 'If I hadn't forgotten the passports, Fred would still be alive and we'd be on our way to France.'

Gemma decided that she wasn't going to get much more out of Mrs Lynch so she left her to be looked after by her parents. But she was going to suggest to the boss that it might be a good idea to have a police officer stay there until they had discovered who shot Fred. Until they knew the motive, his family might still be in danger.

Aled was knocking on doors in Richington Barrow without much success. Close neighbours had heard the bang, thought it was a car backfiring and hadn't bothered getting out of bed to check. That was until he called on Agnes Winterbourne. A lady of uncertain years but obviously elderly, she was an early riser because of her three retired greyhounds which she said needed a good deal of exercise.

'I was walking them down to the sports field so they could run around when I passed a man coming out of the block of flats across the road. He was carrying fishing rods. I thought it was odd because I didn't think anyone went fishing that early and it was much too cold to be standing about on a riverbank. Besides, the river's some distance away. Are you sure you wouldn't like a cup of tea, Constable Williams? I've got some caramel wafers somewhere.' She began to open cupboard doors.

'No, it's all right, madam, thanks all the same. How do you know they were fishing rods?'

'Well, I don't really, but what else could they have been? They were in a long leather bag, like a holdall.'

Aled chose his words carefully — he didn't want to scare the old dear by telling her there was a gunman on the loose. 'It's possible that the man you saw may have committed a crime. My boss, Detective Inspector Dawes, is anxious to speak to him. Could you describe him for me, please?'

'Detective Inspector Dawes? No, I don't believe I've ever met . . .'

'No, madam.' Aled took a deep breath. 'Can you describe the man you saw?'

'Oh, I see. Silly me. Well, he was about your height, maybe a bit thinner, and he was wearing jeans and one of those hoodie things that all young men seem to wear these days. Not you, of course. You look very smart. I like a man in a suit with a proper shirt and tie. It's a pity they aren't worn much anymore, don't you think?'

'Yes, madam.' Aled tried to get her back to the description. 'What else can you remember?'

'I remember I said "good morning" as he passed me but he didn't reply. He looked foreign — sort of swarthy — so maybe he didn't speak English.'

'Did you see where he went?'

'No, I didn't, because one of the boys decided to wrap his lead around a lamppost and by the time I'd untangled him, the man had disappeared.'

Aled decided there wasn't any more that she could tell him, so he thanked her for her help and left.

'Any chance Miss Winterbourne might recognize this bloke if we showed her some video identification?' asked Bugsy. The four officers were sitting in the police car, comparing notes. Bugsy was eating the sausage roll that he'd trousered before he left and had flakes of pastry down his jacket.

Aled shook his head. 'Doubt it, Sarge. She didn't see enough of his face. Sounds like he's our man, though.'

'What happened to the good old days when hitmen wore pinstripe suits, long Italian coats and carried a rifle in a violin case?' asked Bugsy. 'You could spot them a mile away.'

'I don't think I'd been born then, Sarge,' replied Gemma.

Bugsy ignored that. 'And they always left the gun behind.'

'That's a bit risky, isn't it?' asked Aled.

'No, son. The highest risk of being caught is having the gun on you, right after a shooting. It's high risk because it's been fired and there's the smell and gunshot residue. Rifling marks on the bullet in the victim can tie the gun to the crime, so if you're caught with the murder weapon, they've got you. Leaving it at the crime scene cuts the connection, as long as you didn't leave fingerprints on the gun or cartridge cases.'

'If you've finished your lecture on how to be a sniper and not get caught, Sergeant, I think we should take a look up there.' Jack pointed to the block of flats across the road. 'If, as Miss Winterbourne said, our man was carrying a holdall, it's unlikely we'll find the gun, but he might have left something behind that's traceable.'

The lift wasn't working so they climbed the stairs to the flat at the top of the block which Doctor Hardacre had thought to be the most likely source of the shot. Most of the flats were occupied, but this one was completely empty, no furniture, carpets or curtains, and it smelled strongly of bleach. The door was wide open. They trooped inside, being careful not to touch anything. They needn't have bothered.

'Nothing,' said Jack, looking around. 'No cartridge cases, no cigarette buts, no empty drinks bottles, nothing to show that anyone has been in here at all. This sniper's a professional. It's how he makes his living and he won't have left anything behind that might help us catch him. We'll get the fingerprint guys to sweep it, but my guess is that they won't find anything. He's probably on a plane back to whatever country he came from by now.'

'Are you thinking what I'm thinking, guv?' asked Bugsy.

'Try me.'

'A professional hitman like this one will have been hired by someone with contacts in organized crime — the heavy mob. Who do we know who fits that description?'

'Bernie Shakespeare,' said Jack.

'But why Fred Lynch?' asked Gemma. 'He was a farm worker not a rival gangster. All right, he may have gambled in Bernie's casinos, but casino owners don't shoot people who have got into debt. If they're dead, you're never going to get your money, are you?'

'Good point,' agreed Jack. 'It means Bernie wanted Lynch dead for some other reason, and Lynch must have suspected there was a contract out on him which is why he was desperate to get away with his family. Gemma, did you get any indication from Mrs Lynch that she knew what this holiday was about?'

'Not really. She just said Fred told her he'd had a win at the club and that's what was paying for the holiday. If she suspected anything else, she wasn't about to tell me. As far as she was concerned, Fred was the model husband.'

'OK, let's get back to the station and have some breakfast,' said Jack. 'I can hear Sergeant Malone's stomach rumbling from here.'

CHAPTER TEN

The editor of the *Richington Echo* lost no time in reporting the shooting. This was real headline stuff. On his way up the editorial ladder, he'd learned that the duty of journalists is to report the news accurately and fairly, without bias or sensationalism. They must fact-check their information to ensure that it's accurate. He'd also learned that this approach didn't sell papers or get you on the radio and television. Accordingly, his headline read: *Farm worker shot down in cold blood while wife and children looked on.* The feature continued:

> *Fred Lynch, 45, was shot dead on his own doorstep in what is thought to be a revenge killing. This follows the recent discovery of the murdered body of Venetia Adler on the farm where Lynch worked. Wife, Jean, mum-of-two, is being looked after by relatives. Detective Chief Superintendent George Garwood, head of the Murder Investigation Team, declined to comment.*

The editor had paid for a photo of Venetia looking glamorous from an anonymous girlfriend of hers, and plastered it above the feature.

DCS Garwood marched down the corridor and threw open the door of the incident room. 'Dawes, what are you playing at?'

DI Crump scurried up from his end of the room. 'I believe Inspector Dawes is attending to a call of nature, sir. Can I help?'

'Oh, Crumpet, it's you.' Garwood had all but forgotten about him since he'd brought him in to put Dawes' nose out of joint. 'What do you know about this shooting out at Richington Barrow?'

'Nothing, sir. The newspaper report implies it has something to do with the Venetia Adler murder, and as you know, DI Dawes and I are working behind firewalls so we haven't shared any information. My case, the Broadbent murder, is well on the way to its conclusion. Coriander Dawes is obviously guilty of the murder of her ex-husband. It's only a matter of time before she cracks and gives me enough evidence to charge her.'

Garwood hesitated. As well as being DI Dawes' wife, Corrie Dawes was an old schoolfriend of his own wife, Cynthia. They'd known each other for years. Coriander's Cuisine catered all their dinner parties and Corrie was a member of Cynthia's many clubs and charities. It wouldn't look good for the Garwoods' standing in the community if a close friend turned out to be a murderer. 'Are you sure?'

'Oh yes, positive, sir.' Crump's round face glowed with confidence. 'I've had her van brought in for forensic examination. There's bound to be something in there that will prove her guilt. I just need to find it. Then I can present my whole case to the CPS.'

'Right. Er . . . OK. Carry on.' Garwood had seen Dawes appear at the other end of the firewall and strode up there. He waved the station copy of the *Echo* at him. 'Dawes, this rag seems to know more about your case than you do. What does it mean "a revenge killing"? Did this Lynch character strangle Venetia Adler in a fit of passion and then her husband or boyfriend shot him?'

Jack stayed calm. 'We have nothing to suggest that was the case, sir. I've no idea where the *Echo* got this story. All the facts so far point towards an execution by a professional sniper. We don't yet have a motive.'

'Well, bloody well find one, man! We've got three people dead and nobody has been arrested. The commander expects results and so do I!' He stomped off back to his office.

'What did the old man want?' asked Bugsy.

'He wanted to know if the Lynch shooting was connected to Venetia Adler's murder. The backstory implied by the *Echo* is that Lynch did it and was shot in revenge.'

'That's bollocks, guv. Contentious crap to sell papers.'

'I agree. If Lynch was responsible for Venetia's murder, and we'd already decided it was unlikely, the only person who might have wanted revenge is Marco. Teresa Shakespeare hated her and was glad she was dead.'

'Do we know where Marco was the night she died?' asked Bugsy.

'Yes, Sarge.' Clive tapped his keys. 'He was at a party at the Tempest Club. It was Bernie's birthday. The whole family was there, all night, and there's a whole bunch of friends, bouncers, bar staff and call girls who will swear to it.'

'In that case, I think we should pay the Tempest Club a visit. Bugsy, you're with me.'

On the way out of the station, Jack and Bugsy passed the front desk where Sergeant Parsloe was talking to Bert Cook. Norman called out to them, 'Jack, Mr Cook has just brought this in.' He showed him a bank card that he'd placed in an evidence envelope.

Jack took it. The name on it was Frederick Lynch. 'Where did you find this, Mr Cook?'

'It was buried on top of the silage. I turned it up when I was moving some to sell to my neighbour. It must have fallen out of Fred's pocket. I thought it should go back to Jean by rights, but I didn't want to trouble her at this time — she must be feeling terrible — so I thought I'd hand it in to you people.'

'Quite right, Mr Cook,' said Norman.

Jack turned the card over. It still had three years until the expiry date so it wasn't an old one. 'When you say, "on top of the silage", Mr Cook, do you mean near where you found the young woman's body?'

Bert thought about it. 'Yes, I suppose I do. It had been packed down a bit, probably with all those forensic people tramping about up there. The digger on the front of my tractor unearthed it.'

Jack was a little surprised that the SOCO team hadn't found it. It raised the question of how it got there if Fred hadn't been present on the morning Bert Cook had found the body. 'Did Mr Lynch help you, initially, to build the mound of silage and cover it with the tarpaulin and tyres?'

'No, not that one. He was doing some work to repair the fence in one of the fields. Young Darren helped me. He's young with plenty of muscle and can drive a tractor. I shall miss him.'

'Has he left you, then?' asked Bugsy.

'Yes. He's gone to work on a farm over at Richington Warren. He said my farm was too dangerous, what with the young lady getting murdered and then Fred being shot. He said he was scared he might be next, so he was off.'

In the car on the way to the Tempest Club, Bugsy said, 'As I see it, guv, the only way Fred Lynch's bank card could have got under the tarpaulin on that silage was if he was one of the two blokes burying Venetia Adler's dead body.'

'Right. But why? Fred Lynch was a happily married man with two kids and a good job he'd had for ten years.'

'And according to Gemma and Clive, a gambling habit in Bernie Shakespeare's casinos that wiped out most of his wages.'

'So, if he was one of the two men, who was the other one?' wondered Jack.

* * *

The Tempest Club was the biggest of the Shakespeare establishments, and like the others, was lavishly decorated with scenes from the play. A striking mural showing a sailing ship buffeted by a storm covered the whole of one wall. Opposite, the magician, Prospero, and his simple, unworldly daughter, Miranda, were watching the shipwreck from their mythical Mediterranean island. Up above, the spirit, Ariel, flew across the painted ceiling on ethereal wings, while down below, Caliban, the son of a witch and the devil, crawled across the expensive mosaic floor.

Joe was on the door when Jack and Bugsy arrived. He put an arm across the entrance to stop them from going in. 'Sorry, gents. The club isn't open until this evening. Are you members?'

Jack and Bugsy pulled out their warrant cards and held them up so he could read them. 'We're here to see Mr Shakespeare.'

Word travelled fast on The Bard's grapevine and Joe recognized the names of the two coppers who were investigating the deaths of his mate Tom and Marco's girl. He stalled. 'Which Mr Shakespeare do you want? There's three of 'em.' He looked around for someone from management to take over.

'It's Bernie Shakespeare we need to speak to,' replied Bugsy. 'Is he here?'

'Have you got an appointment?'

'We don't need an appointment. Just tell him DI Dawes and DS Malone want to speak to him about the night of his birthday party.'

This had the desired effect. 'Wait here.' He hurried off to find Grant. Nobody was allowed straight into The Bard's office — not even coppers. Especially not coppers.

Jonnie Shakespeare appeared from behind them. 'Officers, I'm Bernie Shakespeare's son. Can I help at all? My father is a busy man and I'm sure I can answer any questions you may have. Please, come into my office and I'll organize some refreshments.' He called across to a young man behind the bar. 'Giovanni, could we have coffee for three in my office, please?'

They followed him into a room that had been carefully designed using colour psychology, eco-friendly elements and ergonomic furniture to disguise its main function — integrated technology. It was equipped with monitors, cameras and surveillance kit of every kind. *That*, thought Jack, *was how he saw us coming.* Jonnie was the club's regulator, a watchdog to anticipate and circumvent any unpleasant surprises.

They sat in two plush chairs on the opposite side of his desk. Bugsy whipped out a notebook. 'I understand your father celebrated his birthday with a party, recently. Can you tell us who was present, please, sir?'

'We all were, Sergeant. My parents, obviously, my brother and a number of our friends. Some of the staff were invited, too. I'm sure, if you ask them, they will confirm it.'

I bet they will, thought Bugsy. *They'd swear black was white if you told them to.* 'What about Miss Adler?' Bugsy scowled at him but he remained cool.

'Venetia? No, I don't think she was there. She didn't much like family get-togethers. She preferred to enjoy the clubs with her own set of friends.'

'But wasn't she engaged to your brother?' Jack wondered what his opinion of the relationship would be. As it turned out, not as vitriolic as his mother's.

'For a while, but I think the engagement had ended by then.'

'Why was that, sir?' Bugsy persisted.

'I couldn't say. Obviously, it's a personal matter. You'd have to ask my brother.'

'We shall need to ask Marco some questions about Miss Adler,' said Bugsy. 'Do you know if he's here right now?'

'No, I'm afraid he isn't, Sergeant. He's taken our mother up to Knightsbridge to do some shopping, but I'll let him know you wish to speak to him.' He smiled. 'Of course, his past relationship with Venetia is largely academic now that she's dead. We were all very shocked when we heard she'd been murdered. Are you any closer to finding out who did it?'

'We're following a number of leads. Was she still living in your house at the time of her death?' Jack watched him but he was giving nothing away.

'It's a big house, Inspector. It isn't always possible to tell who's in and who's out. But Venetia definitely wasn't at my father's party. If she had been, she might still be alive.'

'She was pregnant at the time of her death,' blurted out Jack, hoping to blindside him.

It didn't work. Jonnie remained unruffled 'So I understand.'

'Would you have any idea who the father was?'

'No, Inspector. Your guess is as good as mine. She was a very friendly girl.' He stood up. 'Now, if that's all, you'll have to excuse me. Although the club seems, like the proverbial swan, to run smoothly on the surface, it takes a great deal of paddling by everyone involved to make it appear that way.'

* * *

After they'd gone, Jonnie punched a speed dial number into his phone. 'Marco? You're a bloody disaster! I've just had the police here asking questions about Dad's party. I told them you were there all night. Remember that when they question you, and for Christ's sake, get it right.' He raged inwardly at the injustice of being saddled with an incompetent, self-seeking younger brother. 'Have you any idea how much trouble you managed to cause in just one night? No, of course you haven't! We've got a very important shipment coming up — probably the biggest we've ever handled. There are millions at stake and the last thing we need is the cops sniffing around. Don't do anything else to draw attention to yourself.' He cut him off, unwilling to spend precious time listening to Marco whining that none of it was his fault.

* * *

Back in the incident room, Jack added what little they'd learned from Jonnie Shakespeare to the whiteboard. *Venetia wasn't at the party the night she was killed. Marco and the rest of the family were — all night. Nobody knows the identity of the father of her unborn child. All potential murder suspects have alibis.* 'Come on, team, help me out here. What happened that night that resulted in three deaths?'

'So, you think they're connected in some way, sir, like Velma said?' asked Aled.

'Statistically, it's highly unlikely that they aren't connected,' Velma reminded them. 'It has to do with cause and effect.'

'Now I'm really confused,' said Bugsy.

She stood up and took the pen from Jack. 'Let's start with Tom Broadbent. We know he was a career burglar. A bad one, but he would have considered it to be his profession.'

'That's right,' agreed Aled. 'He wasn't the sort of yob who jemmies open your fanlight to nick a laptop and your milk money.'

'We also know,' continued Velma, 'from the note he sent to Mrs Dawes, that he feared for his life.'

'And he wasn't wrong,' said Bugsy. 'A few hours later, the poor bugger was dead.'

Velma was adding bullet points. 'His personality traits were those of a non-violent, repeat offender, so I doubt he would have risked breaking into Bernie Shakespeare's house unless he was certain it would be empty. Someone tipped him off that all the family would be at Bernie's party in the Tempest Club. It could have been anyone who worked there. I think Aled was right when he suggested that once Broadbent was inside, something panicked him enough to set off the alarms before he could deactivate them. My guess is that Venetia was there.'

'That's right!' shouted someone at the back. 'She surprised him and he strangled her.'

Velma shook her head. 'No, his profile isn't that of a killer. I'm suggesting that he witnessed someone else strangling her. That person saw him and Broadbent knew that from then on, he was a dead man walking. Remember what Sergeant Malone told us about the man who was put in witness protection and was found nailed to his front door?'

'So, the person he saw, aided by Shakespeare's goons, caught up with Broadbent that same night and eliminated him,' finished Bugsy. 'That's the connection between the two murders.'

'Then they dumped his body in my wife's delivery van,' said Jack. 'But there are still anomalies around that. Can anyone explain how the killer got hold of one of her knives?'

'I could have a stab at it, sir,' said DC Chippendale. He ignored the jeers and the flying missiles. 'Maybe they cornered him inside the van. Clive says the CCTV in Eden Park had been tampered with.'

'So, where did all the blood go, Chippy?' asked Gemma. 'Doctor Hardacre says he would definitely have bled out from his injury, but there was hardly any in the van.'

'Speaking of blood,' said Sergeant Parsloe who had come up, unnoticed, from the front desk. 'I've had a call from a Maurice Blake at an address in Eden Park. He says he saw the headline in the *Echo* about a dead body being found in the delivery van of local caterer, Coriander Dawes. It asked for anyone who might have any information to come forward.'

'That was Crump's idea,' said Jack. 'He believes in getting the public to come to him with evidence, rather than the other way around. He says it saves legwork.'

'Well, he has got very short legs,' muttered someone.

'Where is DI Crump, anyway?' asked Gemma. 'I keep thinking he'll appear from behind his firewall and tell us we mustn't discuss his case.'

'He's in the garage with the forensics bods crawling over Mrs Dawes' van with a magnifying glass,' said Norman. 'So far, he's found two Brussels sprouts, a walnut and half a satsuma. Doc Hardacre's fuming. She says if there had been anything pertinent to find, her team would have found it. Anyway, Maurice Blake says he's been thinking about that night and reckons he might have something to tell us about blood. He wants someone to go out and speak to him.'

'Strictly speaking, it should be passed to DI Crump,' said Jack, 'but since he isn't here, we'll take it, Norman. Thank you.'

CHAPTER ELEVEN

Maurice Blake saw the police car draw up outside and watched as two officers climbed out and walked up the path. He put on the kettle. Jack had sent Bugsy and Gemma to Eden Park, thinking he should at least be seen to be observing Garwood's order that he shouldn't have anything to do with the Broadbent case. If there was blood involved, he imagined that was what this request was about.

'Hello, Mr Blake.' Bugsy proffered his warrant card. 'I'm DS Malone and this is DC Fox. I believe you have something to tell us.'

'Yes, I might have. I don't know if it will help. Please come in.'

They wiped their feet, wet from the muddy slush that was lying obstinately all over the town. The small bungalow was immaculate. Bugsy guessed living alone and retired, the old chap had plenty of time to clean.

'What is it you want to report, Mr Blake?' Gemma had sunk down into a vast leather sofa, much too big for the room. She produced her phone to record his statement. Bugsy sat opposite on Maurice's riser recliner armchair. He suspected if he pressed a button, it would either shove him up the bum and propel him across the room or hurl him backwards until he was staring at the ceiling. He didn't try either as he was holding the cup of tea that Maurice had just handed him.

'It's about the blood,' said Maurice. 'It said in the *Echo* that they'd found a body in Mrs Dawes' van. It was her ex-husband and he'd been stabbed with one of her knives and it was kind of inferring that she did it. Well, I know Mrs Dawes — she's a kind, lovely person and she'd never have done anything like that. It said if anyone had any information, they were to come forward and speak to the police. Well, on the night in question, she'd delivered a steak and kidney pudding for my supper. I don't know if you've ever tried one, but her puddings are delicious, full of tender meat and rich gravy and the pudding melts in your mouth . . .'

'Yes, Mr Blake. We know Mrs Dawes runs a very successful catering company, but what does this have to do with blood?'

'After she'd gone, I finished my supper and went upstairs to bed. My window looks out onto the lane that runs along the bottom of the Eden Park gardens and it's quite well lit. I could see blood in the snow — a lot of blood. First, I just thought some animal had been killed by a predator, but I was curious, so I went down to look. There was far too much blood for it to have been a small animal and it looked like it had been dragged then picked up and carried away. When I saw that piece in the newspaper, I wondered if that had anything to do with it.'

Bugsy and Gemma exchanged glances. 'Do you think you could show us, Mr Blake?' asked Bugsy.

They plodded down to the end of his garden, and despite the snow that had fallen since, it was still possible to see that a significant amount of blood had mixed in with the slush.

'I believe we may have found the crime scene, DC Fox,' said Bugsy. 'I don't think there's much point in getting a SOCO team out here. Too many people have tramped up and down this lane, never mind all the dogs and cats. We could take a sample of the blood though. Do you have anything we could use to collect it?'

Gemma went back to the house and returned with a water bottle from her bag. She emptied out the contents and scooped up some of the bloody snow. 'Did you see anybody down here, Mr Blake?'

'No, I'm afraid I didn't. Just the fresh blood in the snow. I do hope I haven't wasted your time, officers, but I thought I should tell someone.'

'Not at all, sir,' Bugsy assured him. 'You did exactly the right thing. If only all members of the public were as observant as you, it would make our job much easier. We'll take this back to the station and have it tested. Thank you very much.'

In the car going back, Bugsy said, 'What are the chances of this being where Tom Broadbent was stabbed and bled out?'

'I'd put my next year's gym membership on it, Sarge,' said Gemma. 'We'll get this sample to the lab and see if they match it to Broadbent.'

'Course, it still begs the question as to how they got hold of one of Mrs Dawes' knives to kill him' said Bugsy. 'And if they hadn't buggered about with the CCTV footage, I bet we'd have seen them stab him, carry him to the van and chuck him in, all while Mrs Dawes was in Maurice's house, discussing recipes.'

'All we need now, Sarge, is the perp and the motive and Mrs Dawes is in the clear.'

* * *

Back at the station, with Crump out of the way in the car pound, Jack was comparing the two storyboards. They each had a significant amount of information on them but DI Crump's were focussed entirely on Corrie being guilty. It was simplistic in the extreme with the decades-old rejection as an implausible motive, the crime scene — her van — and the weapon — her vegetable knife. The case was cut and dried as far as he was concerned. All he needed, in his view, was either a confession or enough evidence to convince the CPS he had a case. Nowhere had he considered the lividity issue, the absence of blood in the van, or the significance of Broadbent having broken into Bernie Shakespeare's house just prior to his murder. On the other hand, Jack's own Venetia Adler whiteboard lacked any record of Marco Shakespeare being questioned even though he was a key person of interest. Jack thought he should rectify that sooner rather than later. He was aware that on the face of it, Marco had a watertight alibi for the time of both Venetia's and Broadbent's deaths, but the word of witnesses in thrall to Marco's father was hardly reliable. He decided to bring Marco in for an interview the next day.

* * *

That evening, Corrie was rather more subdued than usual. She had made pasta for supper which was what she cooked when her mind was too preoccupied for anything more complex. Jack noticed her tearing pieces off the focaccia with some venom. 'Jack, when do you think I might have my van back?'

'I don't know, sweetheart. When I left the station, Crump was still crawling about inside with a Sherlock Holmes magnifying glass looking for clues.'

'What is he expecting to find? I wouldn't mind if he was looking for some evidence that will lead to who killed Tom, but he's just looking for something that incriminates me.'

'I know. Don't worry, he won't succeed. We know where Tom was knifed. Bugsy and Gemma found where he bled out and it wasn't in your van. We're just waiting for the lab to confirm that it's his blood. The team is working on the supposition that all the murders are connected and all three acts lead to a Shakespeare tragedy. Once we've cracked that, it'll bring down the curtain.' Corrie didn't look convinced — not by his explanation nor his clumsy attempt at metaphor.

* * *

Next day, there was activity on both sides of the firewall. DI Crump had finally found something that he regarded as solid evidence of Corrie Dawes' guilt. Percy had been going through the pathologist's post-mortem report and found details of Broadbent's stomach contents. His last meal had been a burger with onions and chips, eaten around midnight.

Police Constable Johnson was on loan to MIT to assist Percy since all the DCs were working on the Venetia Adler case on the other side of the wall. He didn't mind, as he had hopes of becoming a detective constable and this would look good on his CV.

Crump called him over. 'Johnson, here's what I want you to do. Go through the CCTV of all the takeaways in the area that were still open at midnight on the night of Broadbent's murder and find out which one he went in.'

'Sir.' He got stuck in straight away and sat through endless footage of people buying fast food, sitting on the walls outside to eat it, chucking the containers on the ground and kicking cans down the street. It took some time, but Johnson finally spotted Broadbent going in and later, coming back out of Corrie's Kitchen. He showed it to Crump who slapped him on the back.

'Well done, Constable. That's the clincher.'

Johnson didn't follow. 'How do you make that out, sir?'

'It's obvious. Broadbent must have told whoever was working in the takeaway that night who he was, and that he was looking for his ex-wife, the owner. He probably intended to scrounge some cash — it doesn't matter what the reason was. Anyway, after he left, the girl will have rung Mrs Dawes and told her, so now she knew he was in the area. She lay in wait for him and when he appeared, she lured him into her van and stabbed him.' He beamed, happily. At last, the breakthrough he was looking for.

Johnson could see several flaws in this hypothesis, not least that Mrs Dawes was no murderer, but Crump wasn't interested in listening. He had enough, he believed, to arrest and charge her. He hurried off to do just that.

* * *

Jack and Bugsy drove to Eden Park and went through the same security rigmarole as the last time, before eventually gaining access to "New Place". Gemma had phoned the club to be told that Marco Shakespeare was at home, waiting on the delivery of a new car. Once again, Teresa opened the door.

'Not you again. What do you want this time? My husband is at the club and I have nothing more to say.'

'That's all right, madam,' said Bugsy, pleasantly. 'We're here to speak to your son, Marco.'

This put her immediately on the defence. 'Why? What's he supposed to have done?'

'We don't know that he's done anything yet. That's why we need to speak to him.'

Marco called out, 'Who is it, Mamma? Is it the garage with my new Ferrari?'

'Wait here.' Teresa put out a hand as if to hold them back. 'I'll see if my son has time to talk to you.' She headed for the games room with Jack and Bugsy close behind. They had no intention of letting her speak to him first. They took out their warrant cards again. You had to do everything by the book with this family. 'Mr Shakespeare? We'd like to ask you a few questions.'

Marco was gaming on an Xbox and smoking a joint which he swiftly discarded in a nearby plant pot. He looked up. 'Questions? What about?' He pretended to be indifferent, but there was panic in his dark eyes, making them appear even darker.

'When did you last see Venetia Adler, sir?' Jack asked.

'I can't remember. It was a long time ago.' The words came out in an uninterested drawl. He turned back to the Xbox, as if to ignore them.

'But she was your fiancée, wasn't she? Did you break it off or did she?' Bugsy wanted to know.

'She . . . left me.' He was annoyed now. 'She went away. I don't know where. She's dead now, anyway. They found her on a farm somewhere.'

'Leave him alone,' shrieked Teresa. 'He doesn't know anything about that slut.'

Bugsy ignored her. 'That's right, sir. She's dead. She was murdered. Do you know anything about that?'

'No! Why would I?'

'Where were you on the night of your father's birthday party, Mr Shakespeare?'

'I was at the party at the Tempest Club with my friends and family. Where else would I be?'

'Venetia was pregnant when she died. Were you the father?'

'Absolutely not. She was a slut, like my mother said. It could have been anybody's.'

'You see!' shrieked Teresa. 'What did I tell you? It wasn't Marco's.'

'I think we'll continue this conversation down at the station, sir. It'll be quieter.' Jack took his arm and guided him firmly to the door.

'Don't say another word, Marco,' Teresa shouted after them. 'I'm going to phone Gregory.'

When they reached the station, Sir Gregory Munro was already there. He was a tall, imposing man with bushy eyebrows and a booming voice. Gemma had put him in the interview room. She imagined he must be a force to reckon with when he was standing up in court in his wig and gown and lying through his teeth. His record of wins was second to none and according to his chambers, he cost a fortune, but he'd get you off, whether you were guilty or not.

They escorted Marco into the interview room and Sir Gregory stood up. 'Unless you're going to charge my client, Inspector Dawes, I'm taking him home.'

Jack knew he didn't have enough to charge Marco with Venetia Adler's murder. No CCTV, no fingerprints or DNA, no real motive or opportunity and a watertight alibi that put him somewhere else entirely for the whole four hours that was judged to be the time of death. As for any connection to the Broadbent murder, the evidence was even leaner. All the same, Jack knew instinctively that Marco had done it. But it would keep. There was no sense in crossing the best barrister in the country and making himself the subject of a complaint that would probably see him on gardening leave until someone else sorted it out. 'As you wish, Sir Gregory. We simply wanted to eliminate Mr Shakespeare from our inquiries, but he's free to go at any time.'

As they walked out, Marco smirked at Bugsy who smiled back like a benign uncle, while clenching his fists behind his back.

* * *

Corrie and Carlene were in the Cuisine Industrial Unit discussing Christmas preparations with the staff. Business was booming and they were wondering about taking on extra helpers in the run up to the holidays.

'I've noticed that more customers are opting to have their Christmas turkey delivered ready cooked, this year,' said Corrie.

'I wonder why?' Carlene couldn't imagine not cooking your own Christmas dinner.

'One lady told me that cooking a raw one yourself is downright dangerous, never mind expensive. Apparently, the instructions said, *Keep your breast from drying out by covering it with butter then elevate your legs for thirty minutes.* She said she'd been under the chiropractor for a fortnight.'

They were still giggling when, suddenly, the door flew open and DI Crump, with PC Johnson in tow, strutted up to Corrie. He pulled himself up to his full five-feet-one and announced: '*Coriander Dawes, I'm arresting you on suspicion of the murder of Tom Broadbent.*'

'No, that's ridiculous!' protested Carlene, getting between them. 'Mrs D hasn't killed anyone. You've got it all wrong.'

'Excuse me, madam.' Crump pushed Carlene to one side and glared at Corrie. '*You do not have to say anything but it*

may harm your defence if . . .' he frowned, *'. . . if you can't remem-*
ber . . . no, wait a minute . . . *if you haven't mentioned . . .'* He
turned to PC Johnson. 'I can never remember the blasted
words since they changed it. You do it, Johnson.'

Johnson looked uncomfortable. He repeated the cau-
tion, trying not to look Corrie in the eye.

'Cuff her, Johnson,' ordered Crump. 'I don't want her
making a dash for it when we get outside.'

Fat chance, thought Corrie. *When you're the wrong side of
a size sixteen with fallen arches and bunions from hours of standing
cooking, you don't do much in the way of dashing.*

Johnson pulled out the handcuffs. 'I'm sorry about this,
Mrs Dawes. If it was down to me . . .'

'I know.' Corrie held out her wrists. 'It's all right.'

'No, it's not all right!' Carlene was furious. 'You'll regret
this when you find out you've got it totally wrong and Mrs D
sues you for wrongful arrest!'

Crump could sense a mutiny brewing among the cooks.
There were angry murmurs and a group of militant ladies was
closing in around him. He made for the door. 'Come along,
Johnson. Don't hang about. We have to get Mrs Dawes
processed.'

* * *

Carlene immediately phoned Jack. 'That idiot Crump has
arrested Mrs D. What are we going to do?'

Jack was making for the lift while speaking. 'I'm on my
way down to the front desk and the custody sergeant. I'll get
back to you.'

Corrie was at the desk, emptying her handbag and pock-
ets and putting her possessions in a tray when Jack got there.
'Crump, what on earth are you doing? My wife hasn't killed
anyone.'

'You shouldn't be here, DI Dawes,' Crump replied.
'Conflict of interest and all that.' He tapped the side of his nose.

Jack resisted the urge to punch him on it and put an arm around Corrie's shoulders. 'Don't worry, sweetheart. He has to let you go in twenty-four hours or charge you.'

'I think you'll find, DI Dawes, that I can apply for anything up to ninety-six hours in the case of a serious crime like murder, but I doubt it will take me that long to get this case sewn up.' He trotted off to prepare the file for the CPS.

When Jack got back to the incident room, he found PC Johnson talking earnestly to Bugsy. 'Honestly, Sarge, I really don't think DI Crump has enough to charge Mrs Dawes, but I believe he'll try.' He explained how he'd found CCTV evidence of Broadbent going into Corrie's Kitchen and that DI Crump was determined Mrs Dawes had received a tip-off from the girl serving. 'DI Crump says that all he has to do now is find the girl from the takeaway, get her to make a statement confessing that she'd warned Mrs Dawes her ex-husband was in the area, and he's sure the CPS will give the go ahead to prosecute.'

'And I'm equally sure they won't,' said Jack. 'The girl in Corrie's Kitchen that night was Carlene. She was standing in for a colleague with flu. She didn't even know who Broadbent was, let alone that he'd once been married to Corrie. None of us knew he was back on the scene until Carlene brought the napkin round that night, and by then, Broadbent was already dead.'

'Right, guv,' said Bugsy. 'Old Crumpet's going to be left with egg on his face as well as down his tie.'

CHAPTER TWELVE

DI Crump's interview with Carlene was brief — rather briefer than he'd anticipated. He'd sent PC Johnson to bring her in and was somewhat disconcerted to find that she was the same forceful young woman who had pushed between them when he'd arrested Mrs Dawes. And being a stranger to Kings Richington, he was unaware of their very close business and personal relationships. Nevertheless, he was determined to force a statement from her in support of his submission to the CPS.

When it came to MMO, Percy had a tenuous grasp on the *method* — Mrs Dawes had the skill, knowledge and knives to be able to commit the murder. She'd had *opportunity* — the time, chance and access to the victim, thanks to this Carlene person tipping her off, but her *motive* — the reason she wanted Broadbent dead, seemed to have evaded him completely as Carlene was quick to point out. They eyeballed each other across the table.

'For a detective inspector, DI Crump, you don't have much of a clue, do you?'

Percy was wrong-footed. 'Pardon?'

'Why would Mrs Dawes want to harm a man she hadn't seen or heard from for over twenty years?'

He thrashed about for a credible motive. 'She's a woman. They bear grudges.' He felt qualified to comment on such matters as the ex-Mrs Crump had divorced him for nothing more serious than keeping his racing pigeons in the bedroom. He became impatient. 'All I need you to do, young woman, is sign a statement admitting you phoned Mrs Dawes and told her Broadbent was in your takeaway so she could lie in wait and ambush him when he came out.' He pushed the form and a pen towards her. Carlene pushed it back.

'But I didn't phone her. I hadn't a clue who the bloke was, only that he asked for her surname and did I know what she was called before that — and I didn't. Then he wrote a note on a napkin saying he was in trouble and needed her help and asked me to give it to her.'

'Aah!' Crump shot to his feet as if he'd sat on something sharp. His braces twanged menacingly and several ginger hairs lost their battle with gravity and fell out onto his collar. 'Now, we're getting to it. Where is the napkin?'

'I gave it to Mrs Dawes later that night after I'd closed the takeaway. I saw her read it, then screw it up and chuck it in the bin.'

'Because she knew he was lying dead in her van and she wanted to get rid of anything that might incriminate her.' He was triumphant. He pushed the statement form towards her. 'Are you going to make a statement or not?'

Carlene pushed it back. 'Not! Making a false statement could get me six months for perverting the course of justice. Has it occurred to you, DI Crump, that while you're wasting time trying to fit up Mrs Dawes, the real killer is still out there? If I were you, I'd start looking for a proper motive before somebody else cops it.'

She got up and walked out.

* * *

Cynthia Garwood had taken up a new hobby. When her husband George wasn't in his office lording it over everyone, he had his lodge meetings and golf matches with the commander and jolly fishing trips with his chums, so she felt she needed something to amuse her apart from charity work, luncheon clubs and the WI. As a girl, she'd always been good at art. At fourteen, she'd made sculptures of film stars out of pieces of coal. She had to stop when they couldn't get into the spare room because of the eight-foot model of King Kong that was jamming the door shut and creating a fire hazard.

She decided to have a crack at painting. How hard could it be? With Pollyanna-like optimism, she had mentally held a charity auction and sold her paintings for vast sums of money. She imagined famous artists begging her to stage her own exhibition in the Tate. Cynthia never did things by halves. She spent a fortune on brushes and paints, an artist's smock and floppy hat, a wooden palette with a hole to poke her thumb through and an easel, which she had set up outside in the conservatory "for the light".

Having rung the Westminster Chimes doorbell several times with no success, Carlene had gone around to the back and found Cynthia, pondering over a canvas, brush in one hand, gin and tonic in the other. She let herself in.

'Mrs Garwood, I'm so glad you're home. It's Mrs D. I think we need to . . .' She paused, looking at the painting.'

'Hello, Carlene,' trilled Cynthia. 'What do you think of my bowl of fruit? It's very Cézanne, don't you find? I'm channelling the post-impressionists.'

Carlene studied it. 'Why are the bananas purple?'

'Ah. I think I may have got the colours mixed up. You see, you have to match the numbers on the little pots to the numbers on the canvas. It's very tricky. I must have got thirteen and thirty-one the wrong way around.'

'That explains why the grapes are yellow. But really, I've come to ask for your help.'

Cynthia put down the brush but not the gin. 'Ask away. What's the problem?'

'I hoped you might be able to speak to Mr Garwood. He's brought in a DI Crump from another division to investigate the murder of Tom Broadbent, Mrs D's ex-husband.'

'Yes, he did mention something of the sort. It's because Jack can't be involved, apparently. Fancy Tom Broadbent crawling out of the woodwork after all this time. Is Corrie OK with it? I haven't spoken to her for a few days. I know she's busy at this time of year.'

'DI Crump has arrested her.'

'What?' Cynthia sloshed her gin and tonic over the still life, making it look more like a watery Monet. 'That's ludicrous! What possible motive would Corrie have for murdering a man she divorced all those years ago? She was barely out of her teens.'

'That's what I said when Crump interviewed me, but I think I may have made things worse without meaning to.' She explained about the note on the napkin and Crump's interpretation of events. 'He's sending Mrs D's file to the CPS and he reckons they'll give him the go-ahead to charge her.'

'Over George's dead body.' Cynthia stalked across to the drinks trolley and refreshed her gin and tonic. 'Now we have to think clearly, Carlene. Life is full of problems. There's always a solution. It's just the bigger the problem, the longer it takes to find an answer.'

'Well, you'll have to be quick,' said a familiar voice, 'or Crump will have me banged up by Christmas.'

'Corrie!' cried Cynthia.

Carlene gave her a big hug. 'Oh, Mrs D, they let you out. Thank goodness.'

'I've been released pending further investigation instead of being placed on bail. It wasn't Crump's doing. I think he was overruled. I've a feeling it may have been Sir Barnaby under pressure from Lady Lobelia. She's planning a massive Christmas "do" with loads of important people and she's ordered mountains of food. If I'm in prison, it'll be fish and chips all round and I doubt if the commissioner would be impressed. Anyway, I got your message, Carlene, and here I am.'

'Well, now you're free,' gushed Cynthia, 'it's the three Cs back together again and doing some sleuthing. What fun!'

Corrie was looking at Cynthia's painting. 'Why are the bananas purple?'

'Don't start,' warned Cynthia. 'Has anyone got any ideas about how we can crack this case, find the killer and put two fingers up at Crump?'

'We have, Mrs Garwood.' Gemma and Velma appeared from the garden end of the conservatory. 'We got Carlene's email and we've come to help.'

'Sisters under the skin and all that,' added Gemma.

'Combined intellects,' agreed Velma.

Corrie was concerned. 'Oh, how kind of you both, but you shouldn't be here. You're supposed to be behind the Great Wall of China. You'll get into serious trouble.'

'Only if we're caught,' said Gemma. 'And you need somebody on the inside with access to police information and Clive's technology. Velma thinks this whole thing is down to Shakespeare and his thugs. Tell 'em, Velma.'

Velma was peering at the painting. 'Why are the bananas purple?'

'Never mind the bloody bananas!' Cynthia hopped up and down with impatience. 'Tell us your theory.'

'But leave out all the psycho-bollocks because none of us will understand it,' advised Gemma.

They trooped into the kitchen where Cynthia switched on the barista coffee machine and the five of them sat around the breakfast bar on stools.

Velma began. 'Behavioural analysis creates a profile which, in this case, I've used to connect seemingly unconnected incidents, namely the murders of Venetia Adler, Tom Broadbent and Fred Lynch — the last two we can regard as collateral damage.' She took three biscuits out of the barrel and placed them on the counter in a triangle — a pink wafer at the top to represent Venetia, an oat hobnob beneath it for Fred and a Jammie Dodger beside him for Tom.

'In other words,' said Carlene, 'the murder of Venetia was the trigger for the other two.'

'Correct. There was frenzied rage behind the murder of Venetia. It was an explosive act by someone who felt he had been pushed to the brink by the victim. This points to a man who once had a positive relationship with her that had gone wrong.' She placed a dark-chocolate digestive next to the pink wafer. 'Due to the type of murder — violent strangulation — it's probable he has anger-management issues although there was no attempt to rape her, which often happens in cases like this. It has nothing to do with sex. It's when one person wants to exact complete power and control over another.'

'How old do we think this murderer is?' asked Corrie.

'My guess is that he's in his early to mid-twenties, due to the victim's age. Marco Shakespeare is in this age bracket and had been engaged to Venetia. She was beautiful, passionate, ambitious and pregnant. Marco was, by all accounts, infatuated with her. I believe, on the night she was murdered, she told him about the baby and at first he was delighted, until she told him it wasn't his.'

'Then he lost his rag and strangled her,' deduced Carlene.

Cynthia was curious. 'Do you think she told him who the father was?'

Velma shook her head. 'No, and I think that contributed to his anger. He may have grasped her around the throat in an attempt to force it out of her and choked her accidentally, but I don't think so. He was in a blind fury — this man intended to kill.'

'And while all this was going on, poor old Tom broke in to nick the silver and saw the whole thing,' said Corrie, moving the Jammie Dodger towards the dark-chocolate digestive.

'So, he had to die, too.' Cynthia added. 'Some people do lead complicated lives, don't they? Would anyone like a custard cream? This one doesn't seem to have an identity yet.'

'The reason for your ex-husband's death, Mrs Dawes,' continued Velma, unfazed by the intrusion of an anonymous biscuit, 'was that he happened to be in the wrong place at the wrong time. When a victim has an injury to the back, if it isn't in the act of rape or robbery, it usually points to a revenge murder — reprisal for breaking in and seeing something he shouldn't. Something that could get Marco put away for life.'

'I wish Crump would understand that,' bemoaned Corrie, adding a ginger nut to the mix. 'He's totally convinced that I did it out of some misplaced jealousy. Tom and I should never have married in the first place — we were much too young and unworldly. No matter how much you think you know about love in your early twenties, it's only later that you realize that you didn't know the half of it. To be honest, it was a relief when he left and I could get on with my life. I remember thinking that Eva Larsson had done me a favour. She was a magnificent woman, six-foot three and built like a brick . . . er . . . like an Amazon.'

'And then there was Fred Lynch,' observed Gemma, steering the conversation away from love and marriage, about which she knew nothing, and back to the matter in hand, about which she knew quite a bit.

'That was a contract-killing, plain and simple.' Velma was confident. 'A professional hit-man was hired to take him out for the same reason as Broadbent — to stop him talking. All the evidence points to Lynch having been one of the men who disposed of Venetia's body on the silage mound.'

'And he was in massive debt to Shakespeare's casino,' recalled Gemma. 'That would have been the incentive for him to become involved.'

'We've gone full circle, haven't we?' observed Corrie, following the path of the biscuits. 'Back to the pink wafer. It's all about Venetia.'

'This is all very clever,' said Carlene, 'but we're here to find a way to get Mrs D off the hook.'

'I suppose we could just wait and see if the CPS throws it out,' suggested Cynthia.

'The CPS doesn't need to be sure that someone's guilty to take the case forward,' Gemma was drawing on her legal background. 'Just whether there's enough evidence against the suspect to provide a realistic prospect of conviction.'

'Oh cripes! And Crump is certain there is,' bemoaned Corrie. 'And he's going to follow me around until he finds something he can use.'

'Leave it to Velma and me, Mrs Dawes,' said Gemma. 'We'll deal with DI Crump.' She picked up the ginger nut and dunked it in her coffee.

'How do we get close enough to Marco Shakespeare to force a confession out of him?' Carlene grabbed the dark-chocolate digestive and bit a chunk out of it.

'Do we break into the Shakespeare's house, like Tom did?' Corrie ate the Jammie Dodger.

'No, I don't think so,' said Velma, crumbling the hobnob. 'Clive says the security's like Fort Knox and there are too many bodyguards, most of them armed. We don't want to end up with a third eye like Fred Lynch.'

Cynthia stood up and tilted the brim of her hat like Al Capone. 'Listen gang, here's the caper. We infiltrate the Tempest Club dressed as clubbers, and if anyone asks, we say we were friends of Venetia Adler. After all, she caused all this trouble in the first place.' She snapped the pink wafer in half. 'We find Marco Shakespeare, strongarm him into the ladies, stick his head down the loo and get the truth out of the little creep.'

'Including,' said Corrie, 'why he stole one of the knives from my van, stabbed Tom in a lane half a mile away where his blood was found, then put the knife and the body back in the van. That's one of Crump's main bones of contention in support of my guilt, but it doesn't make any sense.'

'In any case, I bet all Shakespeare's men carry their own shivs,' added Carlene. 'Why use yours?'

'Jack mustn't find out about any of this. He wouldn't half be cross.' Corrie could remember how he had reacted on the previous occasions she had "interfered".

'Don't worry, Mrs Dawes.' Gemma tapped her nose. 'Firewalls.'

'We'll wait until we've got it all worked out,' agreed Velma. 'Then we'll tell DI Dawes.'

Cynthia held up her fourth gin and tonic in a toast. 'This is a lightbulb moment, ladies. We used to be the three C's, investigating crimes the police wouldn't touch. Now we're the fearless five, avengers of injustice and discrimination. Gimme a high five!'

CHAPTER THIRTEEN

The mood in Bernie Shakespeare's boardroom was edgy. Six men sat around the Tempest Club conference table with Grant on guard outside the door, to make sure they weren't interrupted. Six men who, together with Bernie Shakespeare, made up the powerful nucleus of the modern UK under-world, their toxic influence crossing regional and even national borders. Each of them, including Bernie, had started their careers in crime as members of gangs — hijacking lor-ries, handling stolen goods, drug-dealing, common assault and knife crime. Now, as the bosses of significant organized crime groups, they'd reached the peak of their profession, proving that cream rises to the top, but so does scum.

'OK, Bernie, tell us how this is going to work.' Charlie Fraser was head of the Fraser Syndicate, a position of swag-gering authority and influence, but subordinate to Bernie in the East London criminal hierarchy — a position he accepted temporarily. Like the others around the table, he was acutely aware of The Bard's advancing age and heart condition and was prepared for the time when he would vie with Jonnie Shakespeare for control of his father's empire. The amalga-mation with his own would make him the most powerful and undisputed king of organized crime.

'Yeah, what's the deal, Bernie? I haven't come all this way to drink your lousy coffee.' Billy "the Biscuit" McVitie had joined his first gang at the age of seven. Since becoming a gang leader, he'd been arrested at least eight times for various offences, mostly involving violence, but witnesses always dropped their allegations. His main income was from the Soho sex trade, where he had purchased a number of properties which he operated as pornography shops and brothels. Once a lucrative business, demand had tapered off due to the availability of most of his porn on the internet and there were sex workers on every street corner, if you knew where to look. The time had come to branch out.

'This, gentlemen, is the investment of a lifetime.' Bernie stood up and walked around the table, handing out Havana cigars. He didn't smoke them himself but it seemed an appropriate thing for a crime boss to do. To accept one was almost an affirmation of his supremacy. 'Shakespeare Logistics are in the business of supply-chain management. We run a system of procurement, operations management, logistics and marketing so that the purchased merchandise can be safely and reliably delivered to the end customer — that's you.' He sat down at the head of the table. 'Jonnie, will you start the presentation, please?'

Jonnie, seated at the opposite end of the table, pressed a button on the underside and a map of the world materialized on the video wall behind them. The men swivelled their chairs around to look at it.

'This map,' said Bernie, 'tracks the journey of our consignment from Eastern Europe to the UK market of which we, my friends, are the prime consumers.'

Using a gaming console, Jonnie activated dotted red lines showing the direction of travel across various countries and seas.

'The shipment is on its way to the Netherlands which is the transit hub for firearms and drugs that are destined for the UK,' continued Bernie. 'I have negotiated the sale with my Dutch counterparts and arranged for the merchandise to be transported in sealed shipping containers. These will be loaded onto private maritime vessels and brought in via the ferry ports. I shall then distribute them to customers in metropolitan areas. London, obviously, but also Newcastle, Sheffield, Manchester and beyond.'

Frankie Silver looked doubtful. He ran an extensive crime group which had so far evaded any significant penetration by law enforcement through a combination of corrupt police contacts and the intimidation of witnesses. 'You're asking for the money upfront. How do we know you won't double-cross us?'

'Frankie . . . Frankie . . .' Bernie assumed a pained expression. 'How long have we known each other?'

'Long enough to know that it's a question that needs an answer,' Frankie croaked in his gruff, hoarse voice. His vocal cords had been slashed when he was sixteen in a razor attack by a rival gang leader.

'That's hurtful,' said Bernie. 'Really hurtful. We're all in the same line of business. There has to be trust if we're going to carry off a deal as big as this.'

Sidney "Semtex" Sykes had earned his epithet from his use of plastic explosives to blow open bank vaults. He walked with a limp due to a butt call on his phone that had subsequently detonated the Semtex device in his pocket and blown half his leg off. Sykes' Firm embraced diversity — the management team included four family members, a bishop and the father of a well-known reality TV star. Like Frankie Silver, he also had serious designs on The Bard's empire, but unlike Frankie, he was not inclined to wait until Bernie was dead before launching a take-over bid. 'Where will the stuff be stored when it reaches London?'

'I shall store it here, Sid, in the secure vault below the Tempest Club, until we can arrange distribution — and payment, of course.'

'How do we know that customs won't intercept it?' asked Vinnie the Vic. He had found religion in prison but mislaid it again after he got out.

Bernie sat down. 'My son, Jonnie, will explain.'

Jonnie stood in front of the map. 'Containers have revolutionised international trade and at the same time, provided ideal cover for businesses like ours. So many of these containers pass through the world's ports every day, that only a fraction can be inspected. Merchandise can be hidden in sealed shipping containers which claim to carry legitimate goods then be sent on foreign-owned ships engaged in lawful trade. Circuitous routes make the shipments harder for surveillance operations to track. Ship owners and even customs officers often just have to take it on trust that what's inside the container is what it says on the cargo documents.'

'You've done your homework,' observed "Biscuit" McVitie.

'You don't embark on a deal like this without making sure it's properly researched,' said Bernie. 'Are you in, gentlemen?'

'Yeah, I'll have some of that.' Mick "the Miller" was known as "king of the tracks" and his East London-based gang ruled over greyhound racing. They controlled the bookies and ensured they kept only a percentage of every pound they made. But dog racing had declined significantly over the years with only two London tracks currently viable so Mick was thinking he'd diversify into weapons and drugs.

'How about you, Biscuit?' asked Bernie.

'OK. Why not?' said Billy. 'Count me in.'

The responses were almost unanimous except for Frankie. 'What kind of merchandise are we getting? I want to know before I part with any cash.'

Jonnie flashed up another screen. It showed a huge cache of assault rifles, machine pistols and handguns and vast quantities of ammunition. The next screen had similar pictures of large packages of drugs of all types, from cannabis and ketamine to heroin and cocaine. 'If you care to switch on the speakers located under the table in front of you, gentlemen, you can listen to an audio inventory of the merchandise. The operatives handling the weapons and drugs will wear surgical gloves at all times and use phones protected by encryption software. Rest assured, gentlemen, we have taken every precaution to ensure a successful venture.'

After the presentation was over, Bernie and Jonnie went into the bar for drinks while Grant escorted all the delegates off the premises.

'I think that went very well,' said Bernie. 'We're about to make a great deal of money.'

'What about Marco?' asked Jonnie. 'Do you want him in on this?'

Bernie drained his whisky and put the glass on the bar for a refill. 'I think not. He's been behaving even more erratically than usual since the business with Venetia.'

'He could have one of his tantrums and scupper the whole deal. It could land us all behind bars,' agreed Jonnie.

'Maybe we'll include him and your mother when it's all over.'

* * *

That evening, Corrie cooked Jack his favourite supper of corned beef hash, baked beans and brown sauce. She disapproved of all the constituent parts — salt-cured beef, beans that came in tins and sauce from plastic bottles, but put together as a meal, Jack loved it — and she was feeling guilty. She had accepted that he could take no part in proving her innocence so she felt wholly justified in doing a bit of sleuthing with the fearless five. Obviously they weren't really going to shove Marco Shakespeare's head down the loo but a bit of snooping around the Tempest Club could turn up some really useful information. Five pairs of eyes and ears were bound to find something.

'Hello, darling.' Corrie put her arms around Jack as soon as he walked through the door. 'Have you had a good day?'

'Not really.' He kissed her. 'How about you? What have you been up to?'

She could feel herself blushing. 'Me? Nothing. Why should I have been up to anything?' She knew she was overdoing it.

Jack smiled blankly. 'I just meant have you been busy?'

120

'Oh, I see.' She relaxed. 'Just the usual Christmassy foody delivery type things. Nothing special. Nothing that you'd disapprove of.' She thought she should change the subject before she really put her foot in it. 'I've cooked your favourite supper. Do you want to open a bottle of something red?'

Jack raised his eyebrows. 'Wine? On a school night?'

'Why not? Especially if you've had a bad day.'

Jack unscrewed the cap on a bottle of Merlot and found two glasses. 'It hasn't been bad exactly, just frustrating. If I'm to have any chance of getting a conviction for the Adler murder, I need to grill Marco Shakespeare, but with Sir Gregory flippin' Munro on his case, and his mother snarling at me like a jackal, it's as if he has a force field around him that I can't penetrate.'

'Is Marco your number one suspect?' Corrie asked innocently.

'Absolutely. He's got the full Monty — method, motive and opportunity. But I don't yet have enough to arrest him.' He took a big mouthful of Merlot. 'Old Crumpet didn't have enough proper evidence to arrest you, so he had to let you go pending further investigation which, of course, will come to nothing. I don't want that to happen with this Shakespeare guy. Once I've got him, I want to have enough solid evidence to charge him.'

Corrie was thoughtful. With any luck, she and the rest of the fearless five might just be able to find some.

* * *

Saturday night in the Richington Arms was always busy. Tonight was no exception. The football match on the big screen attracted the usual mindless crowd — standing on tables, chanting and drinking and yelling whenever there was a shot at goal. Joe wasn't interested in watching the football, not without Tom. But he was there, in his usual seat. Yobs didn't bother him — he was used to dealing with their sort on the door of the Tempest Club at closing time. Mind you,

you got a better class of yob there than when he worked the Hamlet Club, down the seedy end of town. You got some right animals in there. There was one barney when a bloke bit off another bloke's ear. There was blood everywhere. But the pub wasn't the same without his pal, Tom. Nobody to moan to about the weather, the price of beer or the everlasting snow.

Two men were sitting at the bar, deep in discussion. Joe recognized both of them but was surprised to see them together, especially in what was basically a spit-and-sawdust hostelry. He wondered what they might be talking about. When they got up to leave, Joe hunkered down behind his newspaper. Best they didn't see him — but more importantly, best they didn't know that *he'd* seen *them*. Unpleasant things happened to people who saw things they weren't supposed to.

* * *

Outside, the two men exchanged a few words.

'Are you sure this is going to work?'

'Of course it'll work. Trust me, I know what I'm doing. You just do your part like I told you and we'll both be in the money.'

They went their separate ways — one in a taxi, the other in the direction of his car that he'd parked in the multi-storey.

* * *

On Monday morning, the DI Crump side of the firewall down the Nursery End was almost deserted. Only PC Johnson and a few admin officers were in when Percy arrived late. He'd had a nightmare where he'd turned into a cocktail sausage and a grinning Corrie Dawes was about to impale him on a stick. Consequently, he'd overslept and in his haste to make up time, he'd dropped a whole jar of marmalade and trodden in it, wearing his last pair of clean socks. Walking down the corridor to the incident room, he could feel bits of thick-cut Seville orange sticking in his foot, which didn't improve his mood.

'Have you found any more evidence to prove the Dawes woman killed Broadbent, Johnson?'

'No, sir. I followed her movements over the weekend, like you instructed, but she didn't do anything suspicious as far as I could see. She spent some time in DCS Garwood's house, but I believe she and Mrs Garwood are old friends. They go back a long way to their schooldays, so it isn't unusual.' He decided it would be unnecessary to add that DC Fox, DC Dinkley and Carlene were there too. He was certain that Mrs Dawes was innocent, and while he had to follow orders, he didn't have to grass on the people who were trying to help her.

'Well, it isn't good enough, Johnson. We're looking for evidence that's reliable and credible to put before the CPS, while ignoring any facts that might undermine our case. If we don't find something soon, she's going to get away with it.' He whispered in Johnson's ear. 'Tell you what. DI Dawes isn't in yet so I'm going to creep up to his end of the room and see what they're doing.'

Ethel in the canteen had told Crump that when DC Fox and DC Dinkley had come in for a sandwich, she'd over-heard them discussing an "assignment" they had for Saturday night in support of Mrs Dawes. Then later, when Ethel did her shift at Coriander's Cuisine, she'd heard Mrs Dawes saying she wouldn't be in on Saturday evening as there was something important she needed to do. Crump was certain they were up to something and that the "something" was going to take place on Saturday night.

He tiptoed stickily up the room, marmalade oozing out of his lace holes, and lurked by the water cooler, listening.

'We must make sure,' began Gemma, 'that nobody finds the overall Mrs Dawes was wearing when she stabbed Broadbent.'

'Absolutely,' agreed Velma. 'With all his blood on it, it would be vital evidence. Is it safe where she hid it, do you think?'

'Oh yes,' said Gemma. 'Nobody will find it underneath all that flour. Even SOCOs didn't think to look there. Then, on Saturday night, we'll get it out and burn it.'

'I was worried when they brought in DI Crump,' grinned Velma. 'He's such a smart cookie.'

Yes, a ginger cookie, thought Gemma, suppressing a giggle.

'He's so clever and intuitive, I thought he was bound to crack the case and Mrs Dawes would end up inside.'

Percy creeped back down his end, well pleased. 'Johnson, we've got her!' he whispered. 'Her bloodstained overall is hidden somewhere in that kitchen place, under some flour. And on Saturday night, they're going to get it back out and burn it.'

PC Johnson was doubtful. He whispered back, 'Are you sure, sir?'

'Yeah. I just heard them talking about it. Here's what we do. On Saturday night before they get there, we break into that Cuisine place.'

'Don't you need a warrant, sir?'

'There isn't time and I doubt if the magistrate would grant me one. She probably caters his blasted dinner parties. We'll find the flour bin or whatever she keeps the stuff in and get the bloody overall. As soon as we've got the evidence, we arrest and charge her. Have you got that?'

'Yes, sir, but I don't think . . .'

'You're not paid to think, Constable. You're paid to take orders.'

* * *

After Crump had gone, Gemma murmured, 'Did he fall for it?'

'Hook, line and sinker,' muttered Aled. From where he was sitting, he had seen Crump's look of triumph before he squelched off.

'Good. So, Crump'll be out of the way on Saturday night while we hit the Tempest Club.'

'Can I come?' asked Aled. 'You might need some Welsh muscle.'

'Thanks for the offer,' said Gemma, 'but this has to look like a girls' night out. A swarthy scrum-half from Pontypool would spoil our image.'

CHAPTER FOURTEEN

On Saturday night, the fearless five arranged to meet in Chez Carlene before hitting the Tempest Club. The plan was that a small cocktail would be in order as Dutch courage. Carlene, Corrie, Gemma and Velma sat at a table in the alcove sipping porn star martinis and waiting for Cynthia.

Corrie looked at her watch. 'I told her we were meeting here at nine. I wonder what's happened to her.'

'Should I ring her, Mrs D?' asked Carlene.

'No, it's all right.' Gemma pointed. 'She's just coming through the door.'

All heads turned as Cynthia teetered across the bistro on perilously high stiletto heels. She sashayed up to their table. 'Evening, ladies.'

For a few long seconds, nobody spoke. They took in the low-cut, frilly blouse, the black satin skirt slit to the thigh, and the red feather boa around her shoulders.

'Cyn, what *do* you look like?' exclaimed Corrie. 'I thought you said we were going dressed as *clubbers* not *scrubbers*.'

'I know, but when I thought about it, I didn't really know what clubbers looked like. This is the outfit I wore to the last tarts and vicars dance at the Ecclesiastical Temperance

Club. It went down really well so I thought I'd wear it to the Tempest Club.'

'Somehow, I don't think the two clubs are comparable, Mrs Garwood.' Gemma was astonished. She wondered what DCS Garwood would make of it. Talk about non-PC.

Corrie shrugged. 'Well, there's no time to go home and change, so it'll have to do, but for goodness sake, don't bend forward. That blouse doesn't look too robust — no pun intended.'

'How are we getting there?' asked Velma. She had made a supreme effort and exchanged her usually baggy sweater for a dress and cardigan, which is as far as she was prepared to go with "dressing up".

'Taxi,' said Carlene. 'We've had a small cocktail and no doubt we'll have a couple more when we get there. It'll look suspicious if we drink lemonade on a girls' night out, so we'll leave our cars here.'

'Right. Before we set off, what's our agenda?' asked Gemma. Winging it was not part of her nature.

'As we aren't members,' observed Velma, 'I suggest we get Mrs Garwood to distract the doorman while the rest of us sneak in.'

'After that, we have a good look around the place to see what we can find that incriminates Marco,' suggested Cynthia. 'If he's there, I think one of you younger ladies should chat him up. Lull him into a false sense of security then take him somewhere secluded in the expectation of a grope. Then the rest of us will leap out and give him the third degree.' She punched her palm with a fist. 'We need to force a confession out of the little punk.'

'Cyn, you are becoming as lurid as your outfit,' commented Corrie. 'Come on, let's wangle our way in.'

As it turned out, they didn't need subterfuge. When they reached the entrance, the doorman took one look at Cynthia and waved them through. 'He's expecting you, ladies. Have a nice evening.' He smirked at them rather unpleasantly, Cynthia thought.

'I wonder who's expecting us.' Corrie was curious. 'I didn't tell anyone we were coming.'

'Not even Jack?' asked Cynthia.

'Especially not Jack.'

'I expect he's mistaking us for some other ladies,' guessed Carlene.

'Should we split up?' asked Velma.

Corrie disagreed. 'No, I think we should stay together. Safety in numbers. This place has a dangerous reputation. I don't want anyone to get hurt on my behalf.'

As they sauntered in, Cynthia glanced up at the mural depicting Prospero's daughter, Miranda, looking out to sea, her expression limp and vacant. She shrugged. 'William Shakespeare had some very funny ideas about women. It's easy to see he was never in the WI.'

* * *

Jack and Bugsy were sitting by the crackling log fire in the Richington Arms with pints of Richington's Special Real Ale on the table in front of them.

'Where's Mrs C tonight?' Bugsy wiped the foam from his top lip.

'I've no idea,' said Jack. 'She said she was going out for a quiet evening with the girls to cheer herself up.'

'It's a nasty business, her ex turning up and getting himself bumped off like that. It must be upsetting for her.'

'She keeps cooking things. The fridge and freezer are bursting with Yule Logs, mince pies and all things Christmas. No actual meals though.'

Bugsy was feeling peckish — Bugsy was always peckish. 'Shall I get us a bar meal?'

'Good idea, as long as it isn't a turkey sandwich or a pig in a blasted blanket.'

It went quiet for a while, as they wolfed their way through a passable lasagne, then Bugsy spoke. 'I forgot to tell you, the lab report came back this afternoon on the traces of tissue found under Venetia Adler's false nail.'

'Please tell me they matched Marco Shakespeare's DNA.'

'Sorry, guv. Big Ron says the skin and flesh was Venetia's own. She must have been trying to prise his fingers off her throat and scratched herself with those sharp acrylic nails.'

'Bugger! I really thought we had him. And once we get one murder to stick, I'm pretty sure we could get him for the Broadbent killing and involvement in the Lynch assassination. It'll have a domino effect.'

'It has to have been him, doesn't it? If we could only crack his alibi — but nobody in that club is going to go against The Bard.' Bugsy finished the last of his meal. 'What does bard mean, anyway? I thought it was what you got when you made a spectacle of yourself in some boozer.'

Jack laughed. 'It's what they call William Shakespeare. I think it means someone who writes poems.'

'I doubt Bernie has much time for writing poems. The word on the street is that he's gearing up for some big deal.' Bugsy had a number of contacts on the periphery of the crime world who had proved very useful in the past.

'Does the word on the street know what the deal is?' asked Jack.

'Well, if they do, they're not telling. The last thing Bernie will want right now is the police spotlight on him due to his son's indiscretions. According to my snout, there was a big meeting of all the crowned heads of organized crime in the Tempest Club last week.'

'I wonder what that was all about,' said Jack. 'Not a healthy place to be at the moment. We need to keep a close eye on it.'

* * *

'Is the music usually this loud in these clubs?' asked Cynthia. 'I'm surprised they're not all deaf.'

'What?' shouted Carlene.

'We've been here for two hours now,' complained Corrie, 'and no sign of Marco or any of the Shakespeare clan. Mind you, I doubt we'd be able to get near them in this crowd.'

Cynthia indicated a line of sweaty youngsters on the dance floor who were performing some strange ritual. 'What on earth are they doing?'

'I think it's called "The Lawnmower", Mrs Garwood,' explained Carlene. 'You reach out, take hold of an imaginary lawnmower handle, grab the invisible chord and pull it a few times to start your engine. Then you let the lawnmower lead you around the floor. Do you want to have a go?'

'No, I do not, thanks Carlene!'

'And they said the twist was weird,' muttered Corrie.

A tattooed guy in a baseball cap and multiple piercings gyrated towards Velma, grinding and throwing shapes. 'Hey, babe!' he bellowed above the din. 'Nice cardi.' He grabbed her sleeve. 'Wanna dance?' Velma leaned towards him and said something in his ear. He looked shocked and immediately backed off.

'What did you say, Velma?' asked Carlene.

'I told him to "Go away". Well, it was something like that. It was two words, anyway. He seems to have got the message.'

'Perhaps we should explore a bit more,' suggested Gemma, 'before we attract any more unwanted attention. Let's see what's down here.'

They went through a door that was labelled "Staff Only". There were the usual cups and mugs, a coffee machine and on one table, a half-eaten ham sandwich and some crisps.

Cynthia assumed the raised-eyebrow expression that she put on when she wanted to appear superior and well informed. 'Now, you see, a good staff room should have things like motivational calendars — daily reminders that inspire everyone to stay positive. In any organization, whether it's the WI or the Tempest Club, it's important to spread hope and optimism, especially on long, challenging days.'

Corrie pointed to the solitary, well-thumbed calendar hanging lopsidedly over the sink. 'You don't reckon this

December picture of a lady in a Santa costume with a bare bottom is motivational, then?'

'Absolutely not.'

'Now, this door looks more interesting,' said Carlene. 'I wonder where it goes.' The door had "Private. Strictly No Entry" on it. She tried the handle, but it was locked. 'Has anybody got a nail file?'

Cynthia rummaged in her bag and found one. 'What are you going to do?'

'I'm going to pick the lock. They didn't teach me much when I was a kid in care, but I did learn how to do this.' Three minutes later, the door swung open. Carlene flexed her fingers triumphantly. 'Oh yes! I've still got it — the magic touch.'

'Should we be doing this?' asked Velma. 'What if we're caught?'

'We go all silly and giggly and say we were looking for the little girls' room because we're bursting for a pee,' said Gemma. 'If necessary, we compliment the security guard on his lovely big muscles. It's nauseating but it works every time when you're trespassing.'

They had found Bernie Shakespeare's boardroom, with the long conference table and the chairs arranged around it. There was a drinks cabinet in the corner and tasteful sepia prints of old Kings Richington on the walls — except for the one that served as a video screen.

'I think this is some sort of meeting room,' said Corrie.

'It has comfortable chairs,' said Cynthia, sinking down on one. 'That's all that matters. These shoes are killing me.'

'Hey, what do you think this is?' Carlene pressed a button under one end of the table and the concealed console slid out. A key labelled "video" activated the screen on the wall. 'Wow! This is a pretty cool piece of kit. I wonder what else it does.' She pressed a few more keys and the opening credits of a movie called "Octopussies" began to roll.

'Wasn't that a James Bond film?' asked Cynthia.

'Not this one, Mrs Garwood, and it's got nothing to do with cats either. I think you'll find it's a pretty tacky porn movie.' The following eight graphic images confirmed her suspicions.

'This must be where Bernie Shakespeare entertains his cronies.' Gemma was disdainful. 'Pornography — the last resort of sad old men whose hydraulics are starting to fail. Pitiful.'

'That's very disappointing,' agreed Velma. 'I was hoping for something more apposite.' Velma often used words like apposite — her colleagues had become accustomed to it.

'Wait a minute — there are some more options.' Carlene was tapping keys. 'Maybe you can change channels.' A map of the world appeared.

'Oh, good,' grumbled Cynthia. 'Now we're going to get a geography lesson.'

'Probably a good idea in your case,' said Corrie. 'I remember when we were at school, you told the class that Qatar was another name for snot.'

They watched as dotted lines appeared, traversing the world from Eastern Europe to the UK and finally to Kings Richington.

'What do you reckon that means?' Gemma wondered.

Carlene pondered. 'Well, I don't expect it's the itinerary of Bernie's next jolly *mancation* with his criminal pals.'

'I think I know what it means,' offered Velma. 'He's planning to import illegal goods from Eastern Europe and the dotted line is the route they're going to take.'

The next picture showed them exactly what those goods were and the audio inventory coming from the speakers under the table confirmed it. 'Oh my God!' gasped Corrie. 'Look at all those guns.'

'And there's enough dope there to get the whole county stoned,' observed Carlene.

'Somehow, we have to stop this,' Gemma declared. 'It'll mean blowing your cover, Mrs Dawes, because we'll have to report it to the DI. And the National Crime Agency most definitely needs to be informed.'

'I wonder if Clive could hack into this system. He could . . .' The handle on the door at the far end of the room started to turn and Carlene immediately switched back to the porn channel. This was serious. If Bernie found out what they'd really seen, they'd never get out alive.

A tall, imposing figure strode down the room to where they were sitting, now pretending to watch the next porn movie uninspiringly entitled "Thunderballs" and accompanied by equally unsavoury graphics.

'Well, here you all are. I've been looking everywhere for you.' Sir Gregory Munro's booming barrister's voice filled the room. 'What are you doing in here? I was expecting to find you in my usual suite.' He looked at the screen and leered disagreeably. 'Oh, I see. You're getting in the mood for some fun.' He eyed them up. 'You're not my usual Saturday girls. But no matter. A bit of variation adds spice. We're going to do it on the table tonight, are we?' He spotted Cynthia in her low-cut blouse and split skirt, and his eyes lit up. 'I say, you're a bit of a tart, aren't you, sweetheart? I think I'll start with you.' He bore down on her, unbuckling his belt and unzipping his trousers. The other four leaped to their feet, ready to intervene, but Cynthia stopped him in his tracks with a voice cold enough to stun a polar bear.

'You may not be aware of this, Sir Gregory, but your wife is a regular member of my Ladies Luncheon Club. If you come near me with anything priapic, I shall snap it off and send it to her in a jiffy bag. Do I make myself clear?'

His first reaction was surprise which rapidly changed to alarm. 'This isn't right. Who are you? What's going on?'

Gemma was prepared to bet that this was the first time the great Sir Gregory Munro, KC and barrister to VIPs and royalty, had been lost for words.

'You shouldn't be here. I'll have you all . . . removed.' He almost ran back the way he'd come.

'What do you think he meant by removed?' asked Corrie.

'I don't know but I've got a pretty good idea,' said Carlene. 'Come on, ladies. We're out of here before he has a chance to fetch security.' They hurried to the door. 'Someone's locked it. Quick, we'll use the door Gregory came through.' But that was locked, too, and there wasn't time for Carlene to do her stuff with the nail file.

'What about that window?' Velma pointed.

'Oh no . . . no . . . I couldn't possibly climb down a fire escape.' Cynthia went pale and put the back of her hand to her forehead. 'I can't stand heights. I feel faint. You'll have to go without me. Save yourselves.'

'Mrs Garwood, we're on the ground floor,' explained Velma. 'All you have to do is swing your legs over the window ledge and you're only a metre from the pavement.'

Even that was tricky in a tight skirt, and in the end they had to rip it up to knicker level and post her through the window feet first. Once outside, they hurried to the main road and hailed a taxi.

'That was scary,' said Corrie. 'The sooner we report what we saw to the authorities the better, but I think we need to choose the right opportunity. We don't want to have to explain how we found out.'

'I don't know about you lot, but I could use a gin and tonic.' Cynthia was still shaking. 'The Richington Arms is still open.'

They redirected the taxi driver and he dropped them outside the pub.

They shambled inside and looked around for an empty table.

'There's one, over there,' said Gemma, 'right next to . . . the . . . DI . . . and Sergeant Malone. Oh cripes! Leg it, ladies!'

'Regroup tomorrow evening in my kitchen,' called Cynthia, who was the last out of the door due to the skyscraper heels.

* * *

Bugsy looked down at his empty glass. 'I wonder what they put in this stuff.'

'Bugsy, it's real ale. It'll be the usual ingredients — barley, hops, yeast, water, that kind of thing. Why do you ask?' Jack was curious.

'I think I'm hallucinating. I thought I saw Mrs Garwood rushing out of the pub door wearing . . . well . . . I can only describe it as an outfit appropriate to a lady of the night, if you get my drift.'

Jack let out a guffaw. 'What? Cynthia Garwood? Are you sure?'

'Well, no, not really. I only caught a glimpse as she dashed out.'

'I very much doubt it was Cynthia. Unless she'd been to a fancy-dress party. But even then, I don't think she'd choose something that obvious. Knowing Cynthia, she'd want to be Marie Antoinette or Cleopatra. And the old man would never let her go out looking like she was planning to earn a few quid. I reckon you need coffee, old chum.' He went off to fetch some.

* * *

At about the same time that Corrie was making her way home in a taxi, DI Crump and PC Johnson were pulling up outside her Coriander's Cuisine unit in an unmarked police car. They climbed out and switched on flashlights. Crump walked around the facility several times then pointed to a window at the back. 'Break it in, Johnson.'

PC Johnson was decidedly uncomfortable. 'Are you sure we should be doing this, sir?'

'Of course, Constable. If you're ever going to advance to the giddy heights of my rank, which I think is highly unlikely, you have to learn that in detective work, the end justifies the means. Inside this kitchen-bakery-canteen place is the evidence that will enable me to get the Dawes woman convicted of murder. Break the window.'

Crump stood well back while Johnson pulled out his baton and smashed the window.

'Get rid of all that jagged glass, Johnson — I've got to climb through and I don't intend to cut my arse to ribbons.'

Johnson did as he was told and waited for his next order. He was sure this would end badly but Crump outranked him so he had no choice.

'Well, give me a leg up, man. I have many excellent skills, but levitation isn't one of them.'

Johnson bent over while Crump climbed up onto his back and with a good deal of wheezing and puffing, he grabbed the window ledge and heaved himself inside. There was a loud thud as he dropped his torch, followed by, 'Damn! What the hell is this?'

Johnson climbed through the window with ease. 'Where are you, sir?'

'I'm over here. I seem to be sitting in a vat of soup, or something.'

Johnson dipped a finger in and tasted it. 'No, it isn't soup, sir. It's custard. Vanilla custard, at a guess. You split open the vanilla pods and scrape out the seeds, then . . .'

'Thank you, Nigella! If I'd wanted a cookery lesson, I'd have asked for one. Get me out of here.'

Johnson heaved him out and handed him a nearby tea towel to wipe off the worst of the custard. 'Shall I switch on the lights, sir?'

'Good Lord, no. We don't want some nosey plods in an area car stopping to see if someone has broken in. Look for the flour bin.'

They found containers of almost everything culinary but no flour bins. 'They must use flour,' observed Johnson. 'It's in loads of baking-type things. My wife gets through loads of the stuff.' He paused. 'Maybe that's it. A catering company must use vast quantities, especially at Christmas. I don't think we're looking for a bin, sir. I think we're looking for sacks.'

And they found them. In a temperature-controlled pantry at the back. Johnson reckoned there were about forty sacks, piled up on pallets. 'What do we do now, sir? The overall could be inside any one of them.'

'We start looking, Constable. That's what we do. Find a knife or shears or something to split them open.'

'But it'll make a terrible mess, sir. There'll be an official enquiry. We'll be reported to the IOPC.'

'For goodness' sake, Constable, man up and grow a pair. The Dawes woman will hardly be in a position to complain when she's in the nick doing life for murder.' He took a carving knife and plunged it into a sack like a Marine on bayonet practice. Predictably, the flour spilled out all over the floor. 'Well, come on. I can't do this all on my own.'

Johnson took a knife and began reluctantly splitting open the sacks. An hour later, they had torn open all forty and found nothing. The air was thick with flour and they were both covered in it. Crump tried to brush it off but it stuck firmly to the vanilla custard. He stood there, contemplating his next move.

'Sir, how exactly did you get this tip-off?' asked Johnson.

'I told you — I overheard DI Dawes' team talking about it.'

Johnson chose his words with care. 'Is there a possibility that they might have purposely misled you, sir? We've been following Mrs Dawes' movements very closely and maybe she needed to shake us off, so she could follow another line of inquiry tonight.'

'No, of course not! That would just make me look stupid.' He thought about it. 'Let's get out of here. I told you this was a bad idea of yours.'

They climbed back out of the same window, two white figures covered in flour, standing in the snow like a couple of mismatched snowmen. Suddenly, they were dazzled by the headlights of two police cars and a voice shouted through a megaphone. 'Stay where you are. You're under arrest.'

CHAPTER FIFTEEN

'What sort of club are you running here, Shakespeare?' Sir Gregory was furious at being denied his Saturday night entertainment. On Sunday morning, he had stormed into the club demanding to know what had gone wrong. 'My anonymity has been compromised and I was made to look a fool. Those women weren't the ones you usually provide. Not only did one of them know who I was, she runs a Ladies Luncheon Club that my wife, Audrey, attends. If Lady Munro finds out that I don't come here to play poker on Saturday nights, I'll be ruined. I know the law and I know Audrey — she'll take me for every penny she can get. Who were those women and what are you doing about it?'

Jonnie poured him a drink in an effort to calm him down. 'Gregory's right, Dad. We can't allow strangers to just walk in, especially with an important deal coming up.'

'What were they doing when you found them, Gregory?' Bernie was concerned that they had managed to get into the conference facility.

'They were watching some dirty movie. I thought they were warming up, ready for me.'

Bernie relaxed. 'In that case, I think we can take it that they were just bored housewives out for some fun.'

Jonnie disagreed. 'I'm not sure it's as straightforward as that. I've been asking around and two of the women are serving police officers, another two are married to serving police officers and the fifth one owns a bistro. Not your typical bored housewives.'

'You see?' Sir Gregory blustered. 'I told you they were suspicious.'

'Calm down, Gregory. Go home and take your wife out to lunch. I'll make sure nothing unfortunate happens, and even if it does, I'm sure you'll be able to talk your way out of it.' After he'd gone, it was clear that Bernie was more concerned than he'd been prepared to show. 'Do you think we have a problem, Jonnie?'

'I don't know. One of the women, Coriander Dawes, is in the frame for the murder of her ex-husband, Tom Broadbent. She's married to a Detective Inspector Jack Dawes of the Murder Squad. He was here asking questions about Venetia and wanting to know who was here on the night of your birthday party.'

'Broadbent — wasn't that the bloke Marco shivved because he witnessed him strangling Venetia?'

'Yep, that's right.'

'And then he dumped the body in the Dawes woman's van. My God, that boy's an idiot — a complete liability, just like his mother. Do we need to have Mrs Dawes taken out of circulation?'

Jonnie thought about it. 'Not yet. Let's wait. The cops will do it for us if she's convicted. But I think we need to tighten up on security.'

'You're right. I'll speak to Grant. Where was he, anyway, when those women were on the loose?' Bernie took a few deep breaths and reached in his pocket for his pills. 'Doesn't anybody do their job properly around here? Goodness knows I pay them enough.'

'Take it easy, Dad. Remember your heart.' Jonnie poured him a whisky.

* * *

139

The fearless five regrouped in Cynthia's kitchen the following evening as arranged.

'What's our next move?' asked Carlene.

'Speaking as a police officer, I think we should report what we saw to our senior officer and he'll notify the NCA,' declared Gemma.

Velma, as usual, was thoughtful. 'I'm not sure this is the right time.' Cynthia took the lid off the biscuit tin. They stared at her.

'We're not going to do another biscuit scenario are we?' asked Carlene.

Cynthia looked blank. 'No. I just fancied a custard cream. I missed my tea. Why isn't it the right time, Velma?'

'Well, think about it. What exactly have we got to report? OK, we saw what is almost certainly the blueprint of a huge illegal transaction. But that's all it is — a blueprint. If we blow the whistle now, all Bernie Shakespeare has to do is destroy the video, deny everything and put the operation on hold until the heat dies down. He has a lot of powerful people on his payroll.'

'Right,' agreed Carlene. 'He'll just claim it's the ramblings of a few silly women who'd had too much to drink in his club.'

'But we hadn't,' protested Cynthia. 'All we'd had was a few teensy-weensy little cocktails.'

'Yes, but we can't prove that now, can we?' argued Corrie. 'And he can get a dozen witnesses to say we were staggering about, rat-arsed and trespassing. It'll discredit anything we say.'

Gemma could see Velma's point about the timing being wrong. 'So, what are you suggesting?'

'It's risky, but I think we wait until the deal has gone ahead and all the merchandise has been delivered to Shakespeare's premises. Then he'll start arranging distribution,' replied Velma. 'That way, the NCA will have a clean sweep — the whole allocation list, a lead to the suppliers and all the weapons and drugs confiscated.'

'Why is it risky?' Cynthia asked.

'Remember, Bernie doesn't know how much we found out. If we don't do anything and he goes ahead, he'll want to make sure we aren't around to jeopardize the operation.'

'And how will he do that?' Cynthia wasn't sure she wanted to know.

Velma just raised her eyebrows.

'Right, so it seems to me that we have two choices,' decided Carlene. 'We either go with Gemma and report what we saw to Inspector Jack, in which case the cops will be all over it, Shakespeare will postpone the whole caper and we won't be in any immediate danger. Or we do what Velma suggests and keep quiet until the stuff's delivered and he and his illegal logistics company are caught red-handed. Let's have a show of hands. All those in favour of keeping schtum and making sure the guns and dope don't reach the streets . . .'

Everyone put up their hands except Cynthia. They stared at her.

'Oh, all right.' She raised her hand. 'But if I end up at the bottom of the Thames wearing concrete earrings, I shall know who to blame.'

* * *

When Corrie got to the Cuisine next day, she was met by an irate workforce. 'Mrs Dawes, come and look at this.' She followed Joyce into the pantry where flour covered everything like a clumsy snow scene in a cut-price shop window. 'We've been burgled. I found where they broke in, but nothing's been taken, just all this damage to our flour stocks and a vat of best vanilla custard that looks like somebody has sat in it, so it all has to be thrown out. Who would do this?'

'Who indeed?' Corrie sensed the involvement of someone other than mindless vandals, who would surely have taken some of the expensive equipment and flogged it down the market.

'I think we should call the police,' Joyce insisted.

'Better still, I'll go to the station and report it in person. In the meantime, order some more. We can't bake without flour.'

141

When Corrie got to the station, Sergeant Parsloe was on desk duty. 'Ah. Mrs Dawes.' He looked uncomfortable. 'I think I know what you've come about. It's the flour, isn't it?'

'Do you mean you've caught who did it already?' Corrie was impressed.

'My lads apprehended two men as they were leaving your premises.'

'Jolly well done, Norman. So, they've been arrested.'

'Er . . . not exactly.'

'Why not? If they were caught in the act, surely it's straightforward.'

'Er . . . not exactly.'

'So you keep saying. What's the problem?' Corrie was confused.

'The two men — they were DI Crump and Constable Johnson. But it wasn't Johnson's fault, he was just obeying orders.'

'What?' Corrie's voice went up several octaves. 'Why would DI Crump break into my premises and trash all my flour? It doesn't make sense.'

'He says he was following a lead.' He lowered his voice. 'I think you need to speak to Jack. I'll tell him you're here.'

When Jack found her, Corrie was drinking coffee in one of the interview rooms. 'Jack, what on earth's going on? Why has Crump broken open all my flour sacks? I know he's annoyed that I've been released pending further investigation but it's a bit of an extreme reaction, not to say vindictive.'

'He says he received intelligence that he'd find something that would enable him to wrap up the Broadbent case.'

'And did he? Find it?'

'Apparently not.'

'Did he tell you where he got this "intelligence"?'

'No, he just tapped the side of his nose and said "Firewalls".'

'How bloody irritating. Well, I trust I'll get compensation for the damage.'

On the way back to work, Corrie guessed where Crump had got his "intelligence". She remembered what Gemma had said at the meeting in Cynthia's kitchen. "We'll deal with DI Crump" and she'd picked up the ginger nut that represented him and dunked it in her coffee. Corrie grinned to herself. No doubt Crump had been eavesdropping so they'd given him something to keep him busy. No wonder he couldn't reveal his sources.

* * *

Delivery of the shipment of merchandise was very carefully controlled. The trucks arrived in the dead of night with a timed interval between each rather than in convoy, so as not to arouse suspicion. The drivers were all Eastern European with very little English so were unable to discuss the operation in any detail. Bernie and Jonnie directed each truck to the yard around the back of the Tempest Club and watched while the wooden crates were taken down into the vault. It took most of the night.

'That's a superb consignment, Dad. It'll make us millions.' Jonnie looked at his father with concern. 'You're tired. Let's go home.'

'You're right.' He smiled ruefully. 'I'm not as fit as my brain keeps kidding me I am. As soon as this business is finished, I'll retire and you will take over the company.' He put an arm around his son's shoulders. 'You're more than capable and I'll be around to give you advice.' He set all the complex digital alarms on the strongroom until all the lights were flashing red then they left.

As soon as the Bentley was out of sight, Grant came out of the shadows. He was aggrieved, disillusioned and angry. For some time now, he'd done all the dirty work for The Bard and his empire. He'd run protection rackets, dealt with rival gangsters, hired snipers, made bodies disappear — he'd even done time for Bernie — but he still wasn't considered important enough to be included in this, the biggest deal of all. He wasn't even trusted to know the combinations of the strongroom. Well, he would soon rectify that. He let himself into the club and went down in the lift to the vault. It had previously held stocks of gold, counterfeit currency and the trappings of money laundering and illicit finance, but now he had witnessed it being filled with millions of pounds' worth of illegal weapons and drugs.

The piece of plastic explosive in his pocket was harmless until it was detonated. During their meetings in the Richington Arms, "Semtex Sid" had instructed him on its use and explained that it was very powerful, so you only needed a tiny amount for a large explosion. Grant attached it to the burner phone together with the detonator and fixed it to the bottom hinge of the strongroom door. Virtually invisible unless you were looking for it, it shouldn't be discovered before the time was right — when the Shakespeare family was at home in Eden Park and the club was empty. Then, Grant just needed to scroll through the contacts on his phone until he came to the number of the burner phone. When he pressed that, it would trigger the explosion and blow the door off. Sid and his firm would be waiting in the yard to load all the merchandise into their trucks and he, Grant, would then become an equal partner in an organization that would be bigger and more powerful than Shakespeare's ever was. He sent Sid a two-word text. "It's done".

* * *

It was unusual for Doctor Hardacre to visit the incident room in person, but when she did, it was always because she had something important to tell DI Dawes — too important to notify him in an email.

'Morning, Doc. This is an unexpected pleasure,' greeted Bugsy. 'Have you run out of bodies? If you're looking for volunteers, you're up the wrong end of the room.' He jabbed a thumb over his shoulder towards DI Crump's end.

'I have three pieces of information which could affect your ongoing enquiries, Sergeant. It's important that I tell DI Dawes right away.' The pathologist was used to Bugsy's banter, which was usually in bad taste, and she mostly ignored it. She believed people in her job with her kind of responsibilities didn't have time for a sense of humour.

'What have you got for us, Doctor?' asked Jack.

'Firstly, the lab has confirmed that the blood sample you provided from the snow in the lane alongside Eden Park is a match for Tom Broadbent. I examined the site and despite all the traffic that has tramped through, it is almost certainly the crime scene. The victim was stabbed there and bled out, which accounts for the lividity issue we discussed and the lack of blood in the van where he was found.'

'Thanks for that, Doctor, but unfortunately it doesn't explain how Marco Shakespeare got hold of one of Corrie's knives to stab him. And we're pretty certain that Marco was the killer, but we don't yet have enough evidence to charge him. It's mostly circumstantial and Sir Gregory knows it.'

Doctor Hardacre frowned. 'If he's got Munro batting for him in court, Inspector, we're going to have to make absolutely sure of our facts. I've seen that charlatan enable men to walk free simply on a technicality — men who should rightfully have spent the rest of their lives in prison. He's particularly suspicious of forensic evidence — probably because he doesn't understand it. But this second piece of information should give him something to chew on. I re-examined the knife wound in Broadbent's back. We subjected it to a number of rigorous tests in the laboratory and the results, I'm pleased to say, are irrefutable, even by Munro. Broadbent was not killed with Mrs Dawes' Japanese Santoku knife. The knife that severed his spinal cord, penetrating a lung and an artery had a long slender blade with a needle-like point — razor-sharp, vicious and deadly. The primary function of such a weapon is for stabbing people, not slicing carrots. Mrs Dawes' knife was inserted into the same wound after he was dead to put us off the scent.'

'Now that really is good news, Doc,' enthused Bugsy.

'It certainly is.' Jack was relieved. 'The knife was DI Crump's main argument — his only believable argument

— in support of Corrie's guilt and it was one we were finding hard to discredit.'

'His contention that Carlene phoned Mrs Dawes from the takeaway and tipped her off that Broadbent was in the area so she could lie in wait and kill him is nonsense,' said Velma. 'Clive can drive a coach and horses through it.'

'I hacked into Carlene's phone record during the time in question and she didn't make any calls at all and certainly none to Mrs Dawes,' confirmed Clive.

'And the motive he put forward is laughable,' added Gemma. 'No successful woman with a lucrative business is going to give tuppence for an ex who left her years ago when they were just kids.'

'You said there were three pieces of information, Doc,' Bugsy reminded her.

'That's right, Sergeant, and this one will certainly put the proverbial *Felis Catus* among the *Columbidae*. How you use it is up to you, I'm just the pathologist, but it could help you shake up the Shakespeare family dynamics. It's to do with the paternity of Venetia Adler's unborn child. I took DNA samples from the foetus and we already had the DNA of all three Shakespeare men on the database as they have all been arrested at some point — mostly more than once. I was able to match it with a considerable degree of accuracy to one of them.'

'Marco was quite certain that it wasn't him, although how he could be sure, I don't know.' Aled was at that stage in his development when women and their workings were still a mystery.

'Marco was right,' said Doctor Hardacre. 'He wasn't the father.'

'Surely not Jonnie.' Bugsy could imagine the uproar that would cause. Cain and Abel wasn't even in it.

She shook her head. 'No, not Jonnie, either.'

'That just leaves . . .' Jack was shocked.

'Bernie Shakespeare. That's right. The old man was the father of Venetia's baby. Make of that what you will.'

146

'How accurate is a paternity test when the potential fathers are all related?' asked Velma.

'Good question. I won't take up your time with the processes involved, but in this case, I was able to compare the genetic markers from all three potential fathers with that of the mother and the foetus, so the result is 99.99% accurate. Nice to chat with you, MIT, but I must go now. The bodies are stacking up.' She marched off, giving them a quick wave over her shoulder.

Nobody spoke while they digested the information. Then Bugsy asked, 'Are we going to tell 'em, guv?'

'Too right we are.' Jack was emphatic. 'I've had enough of their prevarication — all that vague nonsense claiming they didn't know where Venetia was: "it's a big house she could be in or out" and "she went away, I don't know where", then "we used to be engaged, but now we aren't". Of course we're going to tell them. After all, it's our duty as police officers to keep them informed of developments.'

Bugsy recalled how Teresa Shakespeare had behaved when they asked her if Marco was the father. Goodness knows what she'd do when they told her it was Bernie. He reckoned they should take medical backup — either that or a fire extinguisher.

CHAPTER SIXTEEN

DI Crump didn't take the news about the knife at all well. Jack was unsure whether there was still a requirement for a firewall now that Corrie was no longer a murder suspect, but he had sent him a hard copy of the report in an internal grid envelope, to be on the safe side. Coming so soon after the fiasco with the flour sacks, Percy felt he desperately needed to regain some credibility among the ranks, not to say with DCS Garwood, and now the main thrust of his case — the murder weapon — had been discredited by the pathologist.

Crump also knew it had now been established beyond reasonable doubt that the scene of Broadbent's murder was in a lane alongside Eden Park and not in the Dawes woman's blasted van. This forced him to concede that the new evidence had effectively destroyed his entire case. Coriander Dawes was no longer in the frame as the killer and everything she'd told him was probably true. And now, because he had spent all his time working on the assumption that she was guilty, he no longer had a suspect. There was only one thing for it — he would have to liaise with DI Dawes. The word around the station was that he inevitably came up smelling of roses, however deep the mire. He trotted up the room to the Pavilion end.

'Good news about your wife, Jack.' He beamed until it hurt. 'Of course, I never believed she was a murderer, but you have to go through the motions with an investigation, don't you? I always say you can trust forensics to come up with the goods. Wonderful what they can prove, these days. Time was, you could arrest, charge, convict and bang up your suspect without someone in a white coat coming forward and telling you you'd got it all wrong.' He paused, studying the whiteboard. 'I see you've got Marco Shakespeare in the frame for both murders — Broadbent and Venetia Adler.'

'That's right, Percy. But at the moment, I don't have enough to charge him and I can't interview him without his barrister riding shotgun and preventing him from speaking. I'm pretty sure I can get a confession once I can share some new information with him.'

'Well, if I can help at all, you only have to ask. As public servants, we all want the same thing, don't we? — the villains locked up where they can't harm anybody.' He sauntered back to his desk at the end of the room. Inside, he was jubilant. He had read Aled's comprehensive notes on the storyboard. Marco had strangled Venetia in a rage because she wouldn't tell him who had got her pregnant. Broadbent had been burgling the house at the time and witnessed the murder. Marco had hunted him down and knifed him. But the most useful piece of information was that Bernie was the father of Venetia's unborn child. All he, Crump, had to do was go to the Shakespeare home and drop the bombshell. He guessed the family would implode and turn on each other and during the frenzy, he would get a confession and arrest Marco for both murders. That was how he would regain his street cred as a detective inspector. But he needed to do it straight away and on his own, before DI Dawes got there first.

* * *

It was pitch dark when DI Crump pulled up in front of the wrought-iron electric gates. He wondered why they hadn't

149

opened automatically. Then he saw the sensor light come on above the video intercom. He'd stopped too far away to reach it so he had to climb out of his warm car into the bitterly cold night air. Shivering, he bellowed into the speaker. 'I'm Detective Inspector Crump from Richington MIT. I'm here to see Mr Shakespeare on very important business. Open the gates, please.' He suddenly became aware of two very large, muscular Eden Park security guards who had sidled up out of the darkness and were gripping his arms. They muttered something foreign to each other that he didn't understand and for a brief moment, he wished he'd brought Constable Johnson after all.

* * *

Inside, Bernie and Jonnie were in the study, engrossed in coordinating the imminent sale and payment of the firearms and drugs. Jonnie glanced at the video screen where he could see a rotund little man in a grubby raincoat, trying to struggle his arms free from the guards' vice-like grip. 'I haven't seen him before. What do you suppose he wants?'

'I've no idea but we'd better find out,' decided Bernie. 'Tell Vik and Stefan to let him through. We don't want any trouble with the police this close to finalizing the transactions. I'll speak to him in the living room.' He closed the screen on the laptop to protect the lists of names and commodities on the spreadsheets.

* * *

One of the guards got a message on his radio and they let go of Percy and waved him through the gates. He followed the tree-lined drive and circled the courtyard at the front of the house, parking close to the low granite wall surrounding the fountain. Clambering out by the impressive portico, he rang the bell then stood back a few paces and sat on the wall, admiring the magnificent house. He rubbed the life back into his numb fingers while he waited for someone to open the door. Icy rain suddenly started to pour down his neck and he turned up his collar, hoping the butler or maid would hurry up. It was Jonnie who opened the door.

'Thank goodness. I'm getting drenched out here,' Crump grumbled.

Jonnie smiled. 'That's probably because you're standing too close to the fountain.'

Crump looked up at the stone sculpture of the naked nymph with water pouring down on him from the shell above her head. 'Oh. Yes. I see. Right.' He squelched inside and stood dripping on the expensive doormat.

'Shall I take your raincoat?' Jonnie shook it and hung it on the coat stand. 'How can I help you, Inspector?'

Crump finally remembered to show his warrant card. 'I have come to update your family on some important developments regarding the late Venetia Adler.'

Jonnie was impassive. 'You'd better come through. My mother and father are in the living room. I believe my brother is in the games room, playing on his Xbox. It's rather late for a visit from the police and I'm assuming you don't have a warrant, but I'll ask if they can see you.'

Bernie was pouring himself a drink and Teresa was reading a fashion magazine when Percy stepped into the huge, extravagantly decorated living room. *Who said crime didn't pay?* he wondered, comparing it to the tiny flat he and his pigeons were forced to live in after his ex-wife had taken the house and pretty much everything else.

Bernie glanced briefly at Percy's warrant card. 'Whatever it is you want, Sergeant Frump, could you make it snappy? It's late, I have work to do, my wife is tired and you're dripping water everywhere.'

'The name's Crump, Mr Shakespeare, and I'm a detective inspector. I thought you'd like to know that we have been able to identify the type of knife that was used to stab Tom Broadbent.'

Bernie looked convincingly blank. He looked across at Jonnie. 'Broadbent? Do we know anyone of that name?'

151

'I believe I saw something in the news,' Jonnie replied. 'Apparently he was killed by his ex-wife with a vegetable knife. But I don't see what it has to do with us, Inspector.'

Crump ploughed on regardless. 'Broadbent was the man who broke into your home on the night of your birthday party.'

'I think that's very unlikely,' said Jonnie. 'You've seen our security. Nobody could get in here without us knowing about it.'

'I think you'll find that he did, and while he was here, he witnessed Venetia Adler being strangled.' Crump could see they were getting rattled so he went for the jugular. 'The sad part is, Mr Shakespeare, the young woman was pregnant with your baby.'

Teresa had stayed silent, but now she leaped up and screamed a lot of unintelligible expletives. 'No! The baby was not Jonnie's. He had nothing to do with the little whore, did you, Jonnie? Tell him.'

'It wasn't Mr Shakespeare junior I was speaking to.' Percy eyeballed Bernie. 'DNA tests have proved that you, sir, were the father of her child.'

Teresa screamed even louder. 'You're lying, you horrible little man. I won't listen. The tests are wrong. You forged them. My husband would never have touched that *buttana*. Get out! Get out!'

Crump ignored her and continued to address Bernie. 'Is that why Marco strangled her, Mr Shakespeare? Because she was having an affair with you and he was insane with jealousy?'

Percy never heard the answer. Teresa picked up a large ceramic hippopotamus — one of the ornaments that Jack had found so ugly — and broke it over Crump's head. He went out like a light and lay sprawled on the expensive Persian carpet.

Jonnie knelt beside him, feeling for a pulse. 'Mother, what have you done? You could have killed him.'

'I don't care. He deserved it, coming to our home with his filth — telling lies to try to trick us. As if I would believe that your father had . . .' She looked Bernie in the eye, the man she'd married when she was only sixteen, and she could tell in an instant that the accusation was true. Her fiery Mediterranean temperament boiled over and she flew at him, pulling his hair and going for his eyes with her nails. She had gouged deep scratches down his cheeks before Jonnie managed to pull her off.

'Mother, enough. This isn't solving anything.'

'*Sporco bastardo!*' Teresa ran from the room, sobbing and heaping Sicilian curses on Bernie's head.

'What are we going to do with him?' Bernie indicated the still comatose Percy, while mopping the blood running down his face with his handkerchief.

'We can't let him go back to the station with accusations of murder, assault and God knows what else,' reasoned Jonnie. 'We'll have the entire NCA down on us, asking questions, just as we're starting distribution of the guns and drugs. We're too close, now.'

'Agreed. Tell Grant to lock him in the basement and get someone to hide his car in one of the garages. He didn't bring any backup and he didn't phone anybody while he was here, so my guess is that he's going it alone to claim the maximum credit. I'll decide what to do with him later.' He went to the drinks cabinet and poured himself a large single malt in an effort to dispel the chest pains brought on by an uneasy feeling that his pseudo-respectable, affluent life was coming unravelled. 'I've decided to move the merchandise from the Tempest Club to the strongroom here in this house. The security's better and we can control who goes in and out. The club is open to virtually anyone and with the police so interested, I can't risk a sudden raid triggered by some more random women looking for the ladies.'

'Shall I get Grant to organize it?'

'No. The fewer people who know about it the better. Do it yourself.'

'OK, Dad.' Jonnie complied without argument. After all the evening's turmoil, he'd noticed his father dulling the pains in his chest with pills so he didn't want to give him any additional stress.

'We can't stay here after this, Jonnie. Once the deals are complete and the money's in our offshore accounts, we'll pack up and go.'

'Where to?' asked Jonnie.

'Somewhere the police can't reach us. Abroad, to a country where there aren't any extradition treaties.'

'What about Mother and Marco?'

Bernie shrugged. 'What about them?'

* * *

The ambience in Chez Carlene was as warm and welcoming in the winter as it was cool and airy in the summer. It occupied the entire corner of Richington high street and inside, the décor, designed by Carlene's partner Antoine, was strongly Parisian. But the Christmas decorations were Carlene's project and she'd opted for several sparkling white trees, symbolising purity and peace, decorated with a metallic theme — bronze, champagne and gold combined with royal blue and forest green. The effect was stunning.

Four intentionally inconspicuous ladies were seated around a table in an alcove, chatting quietly while French accordion music played Christmas Carols softly in the background. Carlene came to join them bearing a plate of hors d'oeuvres and a basket of crusty French bread.

'Hi, guys.' She sat down and lowered her voice to a whisper. 'Any news of the you-know-what?'

'Yes, I have,' Corrie whispered back. They leaned forward to listen — five heads huddled together over the table. 'One of my dinner party customers lives in the same part of Eden Park as Bernie Shakespeare. We were chatting while I delivered her *five-courses-for-eight-diners* set menu. She told me that late last night, some enormous trucks drew up outside his house and a constant stream of men marched back and forth unloading lots of wooden crates. Like a colony of leaf-cutter ants was how she described it. They took them around to a back entrance.'

'Could she see what was in them?' asked Gemma.

'No, but she said they had foreign writing on them and they looked very heavy.'

'Well, that's it then, isn't it?' decided Carlene. 'He's taken delivery of the merchandise.'

'Or they could just be having a new kitchen fitted,' suggested Cynthia. 'You get loads of stuff in heavy boxes, especially if you're having all new appliances. Did she say what language the writing was? Some of those smart Scandinavian kitchens cost a bomb.'

Corrie took off her glasses and pinched the bridge of her nose, despairingly. 'No, Cyn, she didn't say what language it was. And I think we can be fairly sure that the crates didn't contain a new kitchen.'

'I'm surprised he's keeping it in his house before he sells it,' said Velma. 'I'd have thought it would have been safer in one of his clubs in town.'

Corrie shook her head. 'Eden Park is safer. You should see the security guards he employs. A mouse couldn't get in there without one of those gorillas pouncing on it.'

'I didn't think gorillas ate mice,' mused Cynthia. It went quiet and she realized the others were staring at her. 'What?'

Carlene picked up the plate of hors d'oeuvres. 'Have another *gougère*, Mrs Garwood.'

'No thanks, but I'll have another one of those puff pastry cheese balls. Delicious.'

'Did your Eden Park customer manage to count how many crates there were?' Gemma asked Corrie. She wanted to get an idea of the scale of the shipment.

'No. She said she wasn't in the habit of spying on her neighbours and after half an hour with one foot on the windowsill and the other on the corner of her dressing table, she got cramp and dropped the binoculars.'

'Pity. Do we tell DI Dawes what we know, now?' Gemma was still uncomfortable about the five of them keeping the information to themselves although she could see the sense behind it.

'Yes,' said Corrie. 'I think Jack is best placed to decide what to do next. But I'm guessing the NCA will want to wait until Shakespeare's customers have actually received and paid for the merchandise, otherwise their lawyers could claim they knew nothing about it and weren't involved in any deal.'

'Once the stuff's delivered, how will they identify the gangs?' asked Carlene. 'Won't they just pass it on to their customers? It'll disperse into the wider criminal network like folding egg whites into cake batter, never to be seen again.'

'You're reckoning without Clive and his digital forensics team,' said Gemma. 'He'll hack into Shakespeare's offshore bank accounts, find out where the money came from and pass it to the NCA. They'll do the rest.'

'Clever,' said Carlene. 'I never thought of that.'

* * *

Semtex Sid and Grant were at the bar in the Richington Arms. 'The shipment's in the Tempest Club, but it won't be there for long. Bernie's sold most of it and is planning to deliver to his customers so we need to move quickly.' Grant ordered another round, oblivious to Bernie's change of plan.

'OK. I'll make the arrangements.' Sid downed his whisky in one. Now the take-over bid was close, he realized he was starting to bottle it. Bernie Shakespeare had a way of finding out if he was being double-crossed and unpleasant things happened to the people responsible. The sooner it was over, the better. Sid knew that once he had all the gear, he'd also have the collaboration of the other OCG heads and then he'd be too powerful for Bernie to challenge.

'Once your trucks are waiting to take the merchandise away, I'll detonate the explosive and blow the door off. Then you load it up as quickly as possible before some busybody reports hearing a muffled explosion to the cops.'

Sid drained his third Scotch. 'You're absolutely sure you set the Semtex like I told you?'

'Positive. I stuck it to the burner phone together with the detonator and attached it to the bottom hinge of the door, like you said.'

What Grant didn't know was that in the general haste to move the merchandise from the Tempest Club to Bernie's strongroom at "New Place", one of the porters had dislodged the device while manoeuvring his crate through the narrow door of the vault. He saw what he thought was just some random person's phone with chewing gum stuck to it, and having been told not to leave anything behind, he'd picked it up and chucked it into the crate.

Grant's phone rang. He looked at it. 'It's Bernie. He wants me at the house to make some copper disappear.'

Sid was surprised. 'I didn't realize Bernie dealt in scrap metal. There can't be much money in it.'

'Not copper as in plumbing — copper as in Old Bill. Apparently he had a visit from one of the filth and Teresa welted him over the head. He wants me to shift the body. I'd better go, but this is the last time he can order me to do anything.' He got up and left.

DI Crump was still unconscious when Grant hoisted him up off the rug and carried him down to the basement in a fireman's lift. He dumped him in the storeroom as instructed and locked the door. As he passed the strongroom, he was surprised to see it securely locked and bolted and the array of flashing red lights meant all the alarms were set. He hadn't realized that Bernie had anything of huge value in there. But it wasn't his business any longer.

* * *

When Percy woke up, it was dark. He was lying on the floor and his head was throbbing like a badly tuned diesel engine. He sat up and put tentative fingers to the source of the pain and felt a huge lump emerging from his sparse ginger hair. At first, he thought he was at home and had fallen out of bed. Then he realized he was fully dressed, and when he reached up to switch on the bedside light, his Robocop lamp was missing. Struggling to his feet, he felt along the walls searching for a light switch. He found one next to the door and snapped it on. The unyielding door handle told him that it was firmly locked and bolted from the outside. He seemed to be in some sort of underground workroom as there were no windows and it had a washroom attached. It was full of the kind of miscellaneous junk that people store in basements — bicycles, ski gear, suitcases, patio furniture and propped up in one corner, an AK203 assault rifle. He wondered if he could use it to shoot the lock off the door but decided against it. He'd spent three days in police firearms training before they'd bandaged him up and chucked him out, and it had taught him that guns are bloody dangerous. It was also an indication that he was still in Shakespeare's house as he doubted if any of the other residents of Eden Park would keep such a weapon in their basement.

The lavatory cubicle was fortuitous because his prostate was telling him he needed a pee. Sometime later, after he'd relieved himself, he felt in his pocket for his phone. It had gone. In any case, he doubted he'd have had any kind of reception in what amounted to an underground bunker, and shouting was pointless for the same reason. Gradually, his memory started to return. As planned, he'd had an altercation with the Shakespeare family in their living room hoping that, in the ensuing chaos, someone would blurt out something incriminating, and he could arrest Marco Shakespeare for two murders. To this end, his last question to The Bard had been to ask him if the reason his son had strangled Venetia Adler was because she was having an affair with his dad. He remembered Teresa Shakespeare having a hissy fit, then everything went black.

With hindsight, he guessed it might have been better if he'd taken PC Johnson with him for backup. Naturally, there would have been no question of Johnson claiming any of the credit had it gone according to plan, but it might have prevented the predicament he was in now. He sat down on one of the patio chairs and for the umpteenth time during this investigation, he tried to work out his next move.

CHAPTER SEVENTEEN

Midnight. It was crunch time. Semtex Sid had positioned his ex-military transport vehicles at strategic points in town with fast and easy access to the Tempest Club. As soon as Grant had detonated the explosive and blown the door off the vault, his men would rush in, grab the goods, bring them up in the lifts and load them onto the trucks. They would then drive in convoy to his headquarters in the East End and unload them. Mission accomplished. If they were clocked by the police, the vehicles, painted in a matt-finish NATO green, would hopefully pass unchallenged.

Sid and Grant were watching from a safe distance in the doorway of an all-night laundrette, across the road from the club. 'How close do we have to be for this to work?' asked Grant.

Sid sighed. 'It's a cell phone, mate. Basically, they're just small, sophisticated radios. When you dial the number of the burner phone, it converts the signal into an electric current, jolts the detonator charge and sets off the main explosive. Boom!' He made an expansive motion with his hands. 'You can be miles away, another country even, and it will still work.'

'You're sure it's safe?' Grant was nervous. Having set the charge himself, he wanted everything to go perfectly. He'd had no experience of explosives while working for Bernie.

'Course it's safe,' Sid assured him. 'It's such a small amount of Semtex, you'll hardly hear it. Just a muffled explosion and the ground might shake a bit, like a mini-earthquake.'

'And it won't affect any nearby properties?'

'Not at all.'

Since this assurance had come from a man who'd managed to blow off half his own leg, Grant had double-checked inside the club to make sure it was unoccupied. While he had no qualms about jobs that included disposing of mobsters who tortured and killed their victims, he didn't want some innocent cleaner to get blown up. Although they weren't expecting a loud bang, he and Sid squatted in the laundrette doorway, shut their eyes and covered their ears — just in case.

'We're ready, Grant. Press the bloody tit and let's get on with it,' hissed Sid.

With a trembling finger, Grant pressed the contact key on his phone marked "detonate".

* * *

Several miles away, in the silent, snow-covered haven that was Eden Park, residents were sleeping peacefully, safe in the knowledge that the ever-vigilant security guards were poised like coiled springs, ready to pounce on any intruders. Only the hoot of an owl, the chimes of a distant church clock and the occasional snores of said security guards disturbed the dark, oasis of calm.

On the stroke of midnight, an almighty blast sent shock-waves throughout the affluent neighbourhood. Dogs barked and birds fled their roosts in panic. People ran into the street in their nightclothes to see what had happened. It didn't take long to grasp that an explosion had ravaged the luxury, seven-bedroom mansion that was set back from the tree-lined boulevard. Speculation was rife.

'It's "New Place" — the Shakespeares' house.'

'Must be a gas explosion.'

'Can't be. They're all electric.'

'I always thought that family was a bit dodgy.'

'Nouveau riche. Pots of money but no class.'

'No taste, either. Look at that ugly great fountain out front.'

'Has anyone called the emergency services?'

* * *

When Jack's phone rang in the early hours of Sunday morning and Bugsy's number came up on his screen, he knew it must be urgent.

'Hello, Bugsy. Can't you sleep? Try counting doughnuts.'

'You're not going to believe this, guv, but someone's blown up Bernie Shakespeare's house. Uniform's already there and they've called the Fire & Rescue Service, but I thought you'd want to take a look yourself under the circumstances.'

'Blimey! We knew he had enemies, it went with the territory, but blowing up his house is a bit extreme, even for the mob. Any idea what caused it?'

'Not yet. They don't know if there are any casualties, either.'

'OK, I'm on my way. You'd better ring DI Crump. We're meant to be collaborating and he's at a bit of a loose end now that his case against Corrie has broken down.'

She surfaced, bleary-eyed, at the mention of her name. 'What's going on, Jack.'

'Somebody's blown up Shakespeare's house. Nothing for you to worry about.' He began pulling on his trousers.

She sat up, suddenly alert. 'Did you say his house? Not his club?'

'That's right. Why?'

'Jack, there's something important I need to tell you. The ladies and I have been doing some sleuthing and we found . . .'

'Not now, sweetheart. This is urgent and I have to go. Tell me when I get back.' He kissed her and hurried out.

162

After Jack had left, Corrie went downstairs and made herself a cup of hot chocolate and sloshed in a generous shot of brandy. She knew from the video they had seen that in addition to the guns and drugs, Bernie was importing a large quantity of ammunition. She had jumped to the conclusion that it was ammo that had somehow caused the explosion. But the plan had clearly shown that all the merchandise was to be stored in the basement of the Tempest Club until it was shared out to the other villains, not kept in Bernie's house. She was baffled as to why he'd changed his mind. As soon as it was light, she would run the information past the other members of the fearless five and see what they thought.

* * *

The aftermath of the explosion was a scene of near devastation, with rubble and debris scattered everywhere and the sound of sirens wailing in the distance.

'Good job the house is set back from the main development,' observed Bugsy. 'An explosion like that could have taken half of Eden Park with it.'

Jack had located the Chief Fire Officer who was directing operations. 'Any thoughts, Stan?'

'Not yet, Jack. My officers are still going over the site. One thing I can tell you, though, it wasn't an accident.' He produced the remnants of the burner phone and bits of wire in an evidence container. 'This is what caused the explosion. Triggered from a distance, in all probability. From the direction that the explosion took, I'd say it was planted in the basement.'

'Any bodies?' Bugsy liked to get straight to the point.

'We haven't found any yet. I understand there are four people living here — Bernie and Teresa Shakespeare and their two sons. It's a big house — four storeys, the basement and several outdoor buildings kitted out as a gym, a cinema and a sun room next to the pool— they could still be in there somewhere.' He strode off to check progress.

A journalist and a photographer from the *Richington Echo* had been quick off the mark and were interviewing some of the bystanders. Jack wondered what kind of story the paper would print the next day. He doubted whether the Eden Park residents had the faintest idea what kind of man had been living among them, never mind the sort of company he kept.

'Did you ring DI Crump?' asked Jack.

'I tried,' replied Bugsy, 'but I kept getting a message saying his phone's out of service.'

'That's strange.'

'Everything involving DI Crump is strange, guv.'

As if to prove Bugsy right, there was a shout from one of the fire officers who was excavating around the back. Everyone watched, mesmerized, as a ragged figure covered in brick dust and with a lavatory seat around his neck, staggered out through what remained of the side wall. For a brief moment, it reminded Bugsy of an old horror movie he'd seen where an Egyptian mummy trailing bandages had emerged from its sarcophagus and lurched towards the crowds. They had gasped in horror, much as the Eden Park residents were doing now.

'Blimey, it's Percy.' The prominent ears were unmistakeable.

Jack and Bugsy hurried to help him but were beaten to it by a couple of paramedics who put a blanket around him and led him to an ambulance. It roared away in the direction of Richington Royal Infirmary, lights flashing and sirens blaring.

'Thank goodness he's still in one piece,' breathed Jack.

'Yes, but what was the daft old twonk doing in Shakespeare's house in the first place?' Bugsy wondered.

'I think I can guess. He came up to the Pavilion end of the incident room to offer help with the case. He had a good look at the storyboard and saw what we'd found out about the inner politics of the family. He wanted to use it to get a result before we did.'

'So, he came here at night, on his own, to face them with it. Bloody brilliant.' Bugsy recalled the lavatory seat around Percy's neck. 'Looks like he was taken short when the balloon went up. A dicky prostate's a bugger.'

'Jack, you need to come and look at this.' The Chief Fire Officer led them around to the back of the house where the masonry was relatively safe. 'My officers found these.' He pointed to a pile of firearms. 'They say there's lots more down in the basement, and ammunition that helped the fire to spread. Also damaged packages that contained drugs. It's one hell of a haul.'

'This is a big deal, even for Bernie.' Jack was surprised. 'You still haven't found any of the family?'

'No, we're still looking.'

'Look no further, Stan,' said Bugsy. He pointed at the Bentley with the tinted windows that was purring slowly through the gates and cruising up towards the house. It stopped just short of the firefighting appliances and Bernie and Jonnie jumped out, flanked by a posse of security guards.

'What the blazes is going on here?' Bernie shouted. 'Who has done this to my house?' Appalled, he looked up at the smoke and the fire officers tackling the flames that were still licking the ground-floor window frames.

'Somebody planted an explosive device in your basement, sir,' said Jack.

'Have you any idea who might have done that?' asked Bugsy.

Bernie's brain was working nineteen to the dozen trying to fathom out how much they knew and how he was going to con his way out of this one. If they'd been down in the basement, they already knew about the shipment. He cursed himself. Why the hell hadn't he left it at the Tempest Club?

'Are your wife and younger son still in the house, sir?' asked Jack.

'What?' Bernie was distracted, desperately trying to think up a plausible explanation. There wasn't one. 'No. My son, Marco, is driving my wife to Gatwick Airport. She's going home to her family in Sicily.'

'Is your son going with her?' asked Jack, swiftly. He believed Marco to be personally responsible for two brutal murders and he had no intention of letting him leave the country.

'No.' He looked at his watch. Marco would be arriving at the airport soon. He had no way of warning him with the police watching his every move. Marco was on his own, now.

Bugsy was already on his phone putting out an urgent call to apprehend Marco Shakespeare at the airport, using force if necessary, and escort him back to Richington police station where he was wanted for a serious crime.

'Right, Mr Shakespeare,' Jack took charge of the increasingly chaotic situation, 'I'm Detective Inspector Dawes and this is Detective Sergeant Malone. We need you and your son to come with us to the station to answer some questions, please.'

'Yes, all right, Inspector. We'll follow you.' He made to get back into the Bentley, a last-ditch attempt to evade arrest, but two uniformed officers handcuffed him and led him and Jonnie to separate police cars.

More uniformed officers chivvied the onlookers back to their homes. 'Come along now, folks. Nothing more to see here. Go back home to your beds, where it's warm.'

* * *

Outside the Tempest Club, Sid and Grant had squatted in the doorway of the all-night laundrette with their eyes closed and hands over their ears for a good five minutes, waiting for the explosion. Eventually, a lady approached carrying a bin bag full of washing. She stepped over them. 'If you're doing a living statue of the three wise monkeys, the one with his hands over his mouth has buggered off.' She went inside the laundrette, chuckling.

They stood up, baffled. 'You couldn't have set it properly,' complained Sid.

'I'm telling you, I did. There must have been something wrong with your Semtex.' Grant looked at his phone to make sure it was working and the breaking local news came up on his media channel. 'I don't believe it! We've just blown up Bernie's house and the stuff was in his basement.'

'You said he'd stashed it here, in the club.'

'He did. I saw them bringing it in. He must have changed his mind and moved it and somehow, the bomb got taken with it. Now what do we do?'

'We keep schtum and deny all knowledge,' warned Sid. 'The police and fire brigade will be all over it like a rash and I don't want them tracing any of it back to me.' He went off to stand down the transport.

* * *

The editor of the *Echo* was on the ball and by Sunday morning, his editorial was available for all to read both in print and online.

> *Last night, a violent explosion shook the exclusive, gated community of Eden Park. One resident told the Echo "I heard some loud bangs, a bit like gun shots only noisier. I came out to see what was happening and the big house at the top of the square was on fire. There were clouds of black smoke and it was quite scary — not what you'd expect in a refined neighbourhood like ours".*
>
> *A statement from the Richington Fire & Rescue Service read: "We can confirm this is an ongoing incident and we would ask that everyone avoids the area for their own safety". Police confirmed they were in attendance to support the Fire Service.*
>
> *Our on-the-spot reporter can reveal that the property damaged by the explosion was "New Place", the luxury home of local entrepreneur and philanthropist, Bernie Shakespeare. At the time of publication, Mr Shakespeare was not available for comment, but it is understood no members of his family were injured in the accident.*

* * *

Very soon it became common knowledge that the police had found a large quantity of illegal arms and Class A drugs in the basement of the Shakespeares' house. The word on the street was that The Bard and his criminal empire were finished. The Tempest Club had already closed its doors and the Hamlet, the Othello and the Macbeth were soon to follow. All the staff had been told not to turn up. Joe, now without a job, thought back to the two blokes he'd seen at the bar of the Richington Arms. He'd recognized them both but had been surprised to see them together. Now it began to make sense. Shakespeare's right-hand man and Semtex Sid. For no other reason than he was convinced Bernie Shakespeare's mob was somehow responsible for the death of his old mate Tom, he decided it called for a few words in the ear of the Old Bill just to even things up a bit. He went into the station and presented himself at the desk.

'Can I have a word with the officer who's dealing with that explosion at the Shakespeares' house? Only, I think I know who did it.'

Sergeant Parsloe's "nutter alert" started ringing in his head. 'Do you want to tell me who you think it might be, sir?' It wouldn't have surprised Norman if the bloke had said Guy Fawkes.

'I'd rather speak to a detective, please. One of the ones investigating Tom Broadbent's murder. I think they're called Dawes and Malone.' He recalled that they'd told him their names when they came to the club and spoke to Jonnie about the night of the birthday party.

Norman took his name and put him in an interview room and Bugsy went down to speak to him.

'Thank you for coming in, sir. I'm Detective Sergeant Malone. What is it that you want to tell us?'

'It was Grant and Sid. I saw them in the pub together, more than once. Now ask yourself, Sergeant — don't you think that's suspicious? Bernie Shakespeare's right-hand man who he treated like a skivvy and Sidney Semtex Sykes, king of the boom business. They had their heads together as if they were plotting something. Then, all of a sudden, Bernie's house blows up. Coincidence or what?'

'I couldn't possibly say, sir, not without further investigation, but we'll certainly look into it.' Bugsy paused, his mind going down another avenue. 'Weren't you the bouncer at the Tempest Club on the night of Bernie Shakespeare's birthday party?'

'I'm a door supervisor, Mr Malone, and yes, I was.'

'Was Marco Shakespeare there all evening?'

Joe frowned. 'There were lots of guests there. Obviously, I assumed Marco was one of them. It was his father's party, after all. But then again, I couldn't swear to it. Put it this way, I was on the door all night and I never saw him go in and I never saw him leave.'

* * *

Corrie called an emergency meeting of the fearless five in Cynthia's kitchen. It was Sunday morning so nobody was working.

'Where's Mr Garwood?' asked Gemma, looking around cautiously.

'He's playing his usual game of golf with Sir Barnaby.' Cynthia put the coffee on. 'He always loses. He says he lets the commander win because it's good for his prospects, but the reason Barnaby always wins is because George is a lousy golfer.'

'Has everyone seen the local news?' asked Corrie, getting right to the point.

'Yep. Bernie Shakespeare's house was blown up last night.' Carlene reckoned everyone in the area would know by now.

'Yes, it's in the Sunday edition of the *Richington Echo*. The photographs look horrendous,' added Velma. 'Who does the DI think is responsible?'

'I don't know,' replied Corrie. 'I haven't seen him since he got a call in the night and left straight away.'

'Well, George won't know anything about it,' said Cynthia. 'He always turns his phone off at weekends.'

'The thing is,' continued Corrie, 'I reckon the explosion might have been caused by, or at the very least, exacerbated by that huge amount of ammunition that Bernie imported.'

'That's right,' agreed Gemma. 'You hear about incidents of explosions at munitions depots. But his plan indicated that he was going to store all the contraband in the Tempest Club, not in his house.'

'That's my point,' said Corrie. 'Why did he change the plan?'

'And who found out and decided to plant a bomb that might have killed his entire family, never mind anyone else in the vicinity?'

'Well, it won't have been any of his cronies in crime. They were all expecting to profit from it, not watch it go up in flames.'

'How about this for a hypothesis?' began Velma.

They all put their mugs down and paid attention. Velma's hypotheses were sometimes hard to follow if you didn't concentrate.

'Let's suppose that initially, he stored it all in his club like he intended. Then, for some reason — it could well have been us, getting in and nosing around — he decided it would be safer at his house, where he could keep an eye on it. Someone close to him, my assessment is it's someone with a grudge, decides to blow open the vault and steal the merchandise. So, this person plants the explosive in the Tempest Club, but unknown to him, it somehow gets moved to Bernie's house. He detonates it but it explodes several miles away. He's probably still trying to work out what went wrong.'

'So, what you're saying is that indirectly, by snooping around the Tempest Club, we may have caused Bernie's family to get blown to bits,' said Cynthia. 'That's ghastly! Even if they are unprincipled, tasteless cretins with the IQ of an ironing board.'

'No, Mrs Garwood, it's the person who planted the explosive who would have been responsible,' argued Velma.

'I think it's time we came clean and told Jack what we did,' said Corrie.

'I agree,' said Gemma. 'The purpose of the exercise was to find something that would clear Mrs Dawes, and with the help of Big Ron and Clive and dear old Maurice, we did that.'

'So, are we all agreed? When Jack eventually comes home, I'll tell him how the cavalry came galloping over the hill and rescued me?'

'Not quite,' said Velma.

'Oh Velma, why not?' groaned Carlene. 'You're not going to give us a lecture on why Freud wouldn't have approved, are you?'

'No. I just think before we do anything that will get us all a reprimand from one quarter or another, we should consider what we've actually achieved. A considerable quantity of firearms and drugs has been prevented from reaching the marketplace or the dark web and all the other places that the NCA are trying to close down. Bernie Shakespeare and both his sons will be looking at long stretches inside, even with Sir Gregory Munro in their corner, although my character analysis tells me he'll bail out rather than be associated with a crime of this magnitude. And thanks to our intervention, several other heads of organized crime will hopefully be identified by the cash they have already handed over. The murders of Venetia Adler, Tom Broadbent and Fred Lynch will have been avenged and DI Crump will have to toddle back to wherever he came from, having achieved absolutely nothing — if you don't count getting covered in flour and being blown up on an exploding loo. So, where is the advantage in confessing to what was, in essence, an inspired piece of private enterprise?'

It went quiet while they digested it.

'She's got a point,' said Carlene, eventually.

'Jack will be ever so cross if I have to tell him,' complained Corrie. 'I started to last night when Bernie's house blew up, but fortunately, he shot off before I could say anything.'

'Legally, we didn't break any laws apart from a bit of civil trespass,' Gemma decided.

'And they all lived happily ever after,' trilled Cynthia.

'Have you finished your painting yet, Mrs Garwood?' asked Carlene.

Cynthia shook her head. 'No, I'm not doing that anymore. It was too fiddly and I kept accidentally dipping my paintbrush in my gin instead of the turpentine. I've decided I'm going to write historical romances, instead. I've nearly finished the first one. It's very good. This genre is very popular, so it's certain to be a best seller. Would you like to hear the synopsis?' Without waiting for an answer, she flipped open her laptop. 'Listen to this. *Sir Maltimus Extract has made off with Squire Weasel's buxom daughter, Phyllis, then lost her to a Turkish mercenary during the Battle of Blenheim. Sir Malty is then press-ganged into the Hungarian navy, loses his leg at Malplaquet, seduces a lady-in-waiting to Queen Anne, becomes a Whig, abducts a Moorish slave girl and returns to his native Suffolk to wed his childhood sweetheart, Lady Diaphanous Golightly.* What do you think?'

Nobody spoke, then Corrie said, 'Actually, Cyn, I think I preferred the purple bananas.'

Cynthia sighed. 'Oh, OK.' She perked up. 'Anyone for a G&T before lunch?'

CHAPTER EIGHTEEN

The duty sergeant put Bernie and Jonnie in separate cells as soon as they reached the station, without giving them the opportunity to confer. Jack formally arrested and cautioned them on suspicion of obtaining and dealing in illegal firearms, just for starters. The charges would come later and there would be many. They were given tea and offered sandwiches which they declined, having already dined on chateaubriand at the Dorchester. They remained in their cells for what was left of Saturday night. Neither got much sleep. Both The Bard and his son had spent time in prison over the years, but the magnitude of this offence was in a different league altogether. But Bernie was confident that Gregory's reputation and eloquence in court would mitigate any sentence he might be given. The sooner he spoke to him the better. Gregory would have him out of this disgusting cell in minutes. With that thought, he fell into an uneasy sleep.

Jonnie's expectations were rather more pragmatic. It was pretty much impossible to pretend ignorance to the charges he knew they would be facing, with all the evidence sitting there in the basement of the house. It was pointless and exhausting trying to work out how such a brilliant plan had gone so badly wrong. He suspected a double-cross at some point in the arrangements and given the explosives involved, it didn't take a genius to work out who was behind it. With his mother back home in Sicily and his brother potentially facing two charges of murder, he wondered how his father's heart would cope with prison.

* * *

On Sunday morning, despite the impossible situation he was in, Bernie was aggressive and confrontational and demanding his phone call. He got through to Sir Gregory Munro's home where a foreign maid answered. Jack could only hear one side of the conversation, but the message was clear.

'Hello? This is Bernie Shakespeare. I need to speak to Sir Gregory immediately . . . What? . . . Of course he'll speak to me, you stupid girl! Just go and get him . . .'

Jack could hear the muffled response on the other end insisting that the barrister wasn't available.

'How dare you! I'll have you sacked! . . . What do you mean, you've been instructed not to put me through? . . . This is outrageous!' Eventually, he gave up and put the phone down, red in the face and furious, having failed to obtain Sir Gregory's services despite blatant threats to inform Lady Munro of his Saturday night "entertainment", which the maid didn't understand, so was unable to pass on.

Bugsy's face was deadpan. 'Shall I get the duty solicitor for you, Mr Shakespeare? I take it you won't be needing legal aid?'

Bernie made a snorting noise like a pig with its snout stuck too far into the trough.

* * *

Gatwick Airport was rammed. Travellers thronged the fore-court — some queuing in long weary lines, others dragging their whining, exhausted children behind them in their lem-ming-like haste to escape for a Christmas break so they could inflict themselves on relatives in warmer climes.

Sussex police had received a request from Richington MIT to assist in the arrest of a suspected murderer. They had easily located Marco Shakespeare's ostentatious red Ferrari Daytona with its elegant, elongated bonnet sticking out well beyond the other vehicles in the car park. They had put a cordon around the drop-off area for the north terminal as a precaution. Marco had just put his mother on a late flight to Palermo. She had been tearful and begged him to follow her as soon as he had finalized the business in Eden Park. His future, she insisted, was in Sicily where her people would recognize his worth and take him into the Cosa Nostra family. But Marco had no intention of leaving until he had received his share of the equity from the illegal merchandise. If he was to live in Sicily, and it looked like that was his best option, he wanted to ensure he had enough money to enjoy himself. Teresa had declined to tell him what she knew about Venetia and who had fathered her unborn child. She knew what effect it would have on him and his hot temper might result in him being harmed. Neither Bernie nor Jonnie would volunteer the information so she would tell him the truth about his father's filthy behaviour once her favourite son was safely under the protection of her family in Sicily.

Marco swaggered across the concourse, dipping his shoulders in a rolling motion and bouncing slightly on the balls of his feet. He imagined it made him look a cool dude and he was pleased to see that hot babes were eyeing him appreciatively as he passed. He was rapidly forgetting Venetia and all the grief she'd caused him and was blissfully unaware that her death was about to cause him a great deal more. He was looking forward to a fast burn down the road in his new car when he spotted the police cordon around the parking area. His first instinct was to run back into the airport and mingle with the crowds, but his escape was blocked by several uniformed police. Panicking, he did what he always did when cornered, he pulled a knife.

Once again, the editor of the *Richington Echo* was on it with the speed of light, thanks to a contact on *Sussex Live*.

This was the kind of news he had been born to report, not complaints about pot holes in the road or a deacon caught exposing himself in Pizza Hut.

> *A local man has been detained at Gatwick Airport as police deal with an incident involving an attack with a bladed article. An inside source told the Echo that the man is thought to be Marco Shakespeare, the younger son of Bernie Shakespeare whose house was destroyed by fire during the night. It is understood that all three Shakespeare men are now in custody and helping the police with their enquiries.*

* * *

'Where's Gregory?' demanded Marco. 'I'm not saying anything until Gregory gets here.'

Sergeant Parsloe was putting Marco's Rolex, two diamond signet rings, a heavy gold chain and a bracelet in a tray. He'd already exchanged his expensive leather jacket and designer jeans for a grey tracksuit prior to locking him in a cell. 'Sir Gregory isn't coming, sir,' Norman informed him with some degree of satisfaction. 'You're being allocated a duty solicitor.'

'What? That's rubbish! Where's my father? I demand to speak to my father.'

'He's being interviewed and your brother's in a cell further down the custody suite, sir. You'll see them when DI Dawes says you can. Now, be quiet and behave yourself and I'll bring you a cup of tea.' Norman had had enough of young blokes with more money than sense throwing their weight about simply because they could get away with it. This one had been kicking off ever since he'd arrived under escort by the Sussex police. They'd handed over the bladed article that he'd threatened them with. It had a long slender blade with a needle-like point — razor-sharp, vicious and deadly.

* * *

176

'How did you get those scratches on your face, Mr Shakespeare?' Jack and Bugsy sat on one side of the table and Bernie on the other, flanked by a nervous-looking solicitor. Unlike the ingenuous residents of Eden Park, he knew exactly who he'd been brought in to represent and half expected he'd find a horse's head in his bed if he put a foot wrong. Everyone in the law industry knew that the invincible Sir Gregory Munro was The Bard's brief, so why wasn't he here now? There had to be a good reason, most likely to do with self-preservation.

Aled had been drafted in to work the digital recording machine and was fascinated to be in the same room as a real, live gangster. Gemma and Velma had filled him in on what they'd discovered during their sleuthing escapade. He couldn't wait to tell his mum back in Pontypool who steadfastly believed he was in *Traff-Pol*, wearing a pointy helmet and directing traffic.

'I walked into some brambles, not that it's any of your business,' Shakespeare snarled.

'Would you like the police doctor to take a look at it?' asked Bugsy, pleasantly. 'That kind of injury can become infected.'

'No, I wouldn't! Let's just get on with it, shall we?'

'As you wish,' said Jack. 'When the Fire & Rescue Services were dealing with the explosion in your house, they found a very large quantity of firearms and drugs in your strongroom. Can you tell us how they came to be in your possession?'

'I've no idea. I'd never seen them before. I can only assume they were planted there by someone who wants me out of the way. Probably set up by my wife — she comes from a long line of criminals. Her father is a *consigliere* in Sicily.' He took a sip of the coffee he'd been given, pulled a face and pushed it away. 'I understand your wife is not above suspicion either, Inspector.'

'Excuse me?' Jack was taken by surprise.

'I heard she'd been arrested for the murder of her ex-husband,' he sneered, nastily.

Jack bridled but didn't rise to the taunt. He had no intention of discussing Corrie with this man. 'Where had you and your son, Jonnie, been the night your house caught fire?'

'We were dining at The Dorchester. As I have already explained, my other son, Marco, was taking my wife to the airport, so Jonnie and I went out for a meal.' He had a sudden disturbing thought. Marco was a loose cannon, likely to say anything. He didn't want him talking to the police now that they didn't have Gregory to shut him up. 'Has Marco returned safely from Gatwick yet?'

'Oh yes, sir,' replied Bugsy. 'He had a police escort, all the way.'

Bernie blanched. 'Where is he now?'

'He's in a cell down the corridor.'

'Why? Why have you arrested him? He hasn't done anything!' Bernie was panicking inwardly. *Goodness only knows what the idiot has told them. He hasn't the sense to keep his mouth shut.*

'Well for a start,' announced Bugsy, 'he threatened police officers with a rather nasty-looking knife. Funnily enough, the blade looked a lot like the one that was used in a murder that we're investigating. It's with the laboratory now, being tested. If there's even a hint of blood on it, they have the equipment that will find it and examine it for DNA.'

Bernie put a hand to his chest. 'I need my heart pills. They were taken from me when I was arrested.'

Bugsy went to fetch them. Deaths in police custody were rare in Richington and he didn't want to tempt fate.

Aled announced, 'For the benefit of the tape, Sergeant Malone has left the room.'

'Why aren't you out there, looking for the people who blew up my house?' demanded Shakespeare. Thoughts were buzzing around his brain like angry bees in a hive. *This has Semtex Sid written all over it. He's wanted my territory for years — but why sabotage the deal of a lifetime? One where we were all going to make a great deal of money. And how did he know I'd moved the shipment to my house after I'd told everyone I was going to store it in the club? It doesn't make sense.*

Bugsy came back with the pills and the police surgeon. He examined Bernie briefly then turned to Jack. 'This man

178

isn't well enough to be questioned further. He needs to be moved to somewhere comfortable where he can lie down.'

It's a foolish copper who disregards the advice of the police quack, thought Bugsy. Jack was anything but foolish so he allowed Bernie to be led away to rest in a First Aid room with a couch, set aside for the purpose. The solicitor felt he could do with a lie down too. He wondered what the going rate was for early retirement on the grounds of a nervous breakdown brought on by sheer bloody terror.

'Do you want to question Jonnie Shakespeare now, guv?'

Jack thought about it. 'No, he'll keep. I doubt whether we'll get much out of him anyway. He's too smart and cunning, even without Sir Gregory. Let's talk to Marco. Change the tape, please, Aled.'

It wasn't just the tape that changed — it was the vibe in the whole room. When the constable opened the door to escort Marco, he shot in like the cork from a bottle of champagne and bounded about the room in his tracksuit like a hyperactive toddler.

'Would you like to sit down, please, Mr Shakespeare?' asked Jack.

'No, I bloody well wouldn't! Where's Gregory?'

'Sir Gregory isn't acting for you today,' said the lady who had followed him in at a more leisurely pace. 'I am. My name is Hermione Timms. Please sit down, Mr Shakespeare.' She wore a purple parka, red combat trousers and a tartan scarf wound twice around her neck but still long enough to reach the floor. Aviator glasses held down a mop of frizzy curls on top of her head like a hairband. When she pulled a laptop from her outsize shoulder bag, two avocados came with it and rolled across the floor. Wordlessly, the uniformed constable on the door picked them up and handed them back. She nodded her thanks.

Marco didn't even try to hide his contempt. 'Is this some kind of joke? I need a brief who can get me out of here, not a bag lady.'

Miss Timms ignored that. 'What exactly has my client been charged with, Inspector Dawes?'

'At the moment, threatening behaviour with a bladed article, but I suspect more charges may emerge once Mr Shakespeare has been questioned and the lab has had time to examine the knife.'

'Perhaps we could make a start on the initial charge, to give me a feel for the situation, then if further charges become apparent, I shall want time to speak to my client alone.'

'Yes, of course, Miss Timms.' Jack wondered if she was as eccentric as she liked to appear. He suspected not.

'Mr Shakespeare,' began Bugsy, 'when the laboratory examines your knife, are they likely to find blood on it? What I mean is, have you stabbed anybody with it recently?'

'No, of course not!' He looked at Miss Timms. 'Do I have to answer these stupid questions? This old bloke doesn't know what he's talking about.'

'So, why do you carry it when you know it's an offence?' asked Jack.

'To defend myself. The city's a dangerous place.' He narrowed his eyes, believing it made him look hard, like Maverick from Top Gun.

'Did your fiancée know you carried a knife?' asked Jack innocently.

'What does it matter? She's dead.'

'That's right. She was strangled. You were aware that she was pregnant when she died?'

'Yes. What's that got to do with anything? It wasn't mine. I told you that before, when you came to the house trying to cause trouble.'

'That's right, it wasn't yours. If it had lived, the child she was carrying would have been your half-brother or sister.' Jack waited while Marco slowly worked it out.

'No . . . no, it wouldn't. How could it? That would mean Papà and Venetia were . . .'

'At it — behind your back,' said Bugsy, bluntly. 'That's right, Mr Shakespeare.'

'I don't believe you.' He jumped up, furious. 'It's a filthy lie.' He realized now why Venetia had refused to tell him, even with his hands around her throat, squeezing the life from her.

'DNA doesn't lie,' Jack assured him. 'Would you like to see the report?'

Hermione Timms intervened. 'I think this would be a good time for a break so I can consult with my client, Inspector.' The way things were panning out, this was going to be a long day.

* * *

Jack, Bugsy and Aled congregated in the room next door while Miss Timms calmed him down, if that was possible. They could hear him shouting.

'Blimey, sir, that was a bit lively.' Aled was impressed. 'I don't reckon he knew that his dad and his fiancée were shagging behind his back, do you?'

'No, DC Williams, I'm sure he didn't, although I wouldn't have put it in quite such graphic terms.'

'D'you reckon he'll cough, now that he's had some of the cockiness knocked out of him?' asked Bugsy.

'Not if Miss Timms has anything to do with it. When we go back in, I'll tell her that the lab has found evidence of blood on Marco's knife and we're about to charge her client with at least one murder.'

Jack showed Bugsy a note that the constable had just passed him. Big Ron and her team had pulled out all the stops and had indeed found a tiny droplet of blood where the blade joined the handle. Marco had obviously attempted to clean it, but nothing escaped Big Ron. The blood was Broadbent's.

'They'll counter with his allegedly waterproof alibi that he was at the party all that night with scores of witnesses who will swear to it,' said Jack, 'then we'll tell him we've found the door supervisor who'll swear that he didn't see him go in or out all night.'

After about half an hour, Miss Timms came out to tell Jack that they were ready to resume. It was the worst possible timing because at that moment, Bernie was being escorted back down the corridor to his cell from the First Aid room where he had been resting. As soon as Marco spotted his father through the open door, he leaped up, shoved the constable out of the way and flew at Bernie, knocking him to the floor.

'You filthy old bastard! You forced yourself on Venetia — got her pregnant.' Marco knelt on his chest and grabbed him around the neck. 'You knew she belonged to me but you had to have her, didn't you?' He banged his head on the floor several times. 'I'll kill you! I'll kill you!'

The constable sprang forward and pulled him off, struggling and foaming at the mouth with uncontrolled rage. Bernie should have left it there but he staggered to his feet and taunted his son.

'I didn't need to force her — it was Venetia who seduced me. She came to me one night in my study, wearing one of those short skirts and a skimpy top with her breasts spilling out, smelling of perfume and licking her lips. She made it quite clear what she wanted.'

'I don't believe you!' screamed Marco, trying to break free. 'You're lying! She'd never have done that.'

'Oh, but she did — at least once a week. She said she wanted a real man, someone who commanded respect, not a stupid boy who . . .' Bernie went pale and clutched his chest. He sank to his knees, gasping.

Jack took charge. 'Get him out of here,' he told the constable holding Marco. 'Aled, get the police surgeon, quickly!'

By the time the ambulance arrived, Bernie was unconscious, despite some surprisingly efficient first aid, administered by Miss Timms and the police surgeon. The paramedics stabilized him and took him away on a stretcher.

CHAPTER NINETEEN

'Honestly, Corrie, it all happened so fast.' Jack helped himself to another slice of Christmas pie. It was one of Corrie's festive obsessions and although Jack reckoned it had weird things in it, like cranberries, chestnuts and apricots, it also had chicken and sausage meat so he reckoned that was as close as he was going to get to actual food. 'One minute, father and son were at each other's throats, brawling on the floor, next thing, Bernie was on a stretcher on his way to the ICU at Richington Infirmary and Marco was hyperventilating with temper and being counselled by a brief who looked like she belonged in an episode of Dr Who. It was surreal.'

Corrie poured him another beer. 'What about the other son — Jonnie?'

'He's saying nothing. I believe he's the brains behind a lot of The Bard's recent activities and he's tipped to take over — sooner rather than later, now that Bernie's incapacitated. But if I can't find anything to implicate him, he'll claim he knew nothing and all the dishonest dealings were down to his father, and I'll have to let him go.'

'Yes, but on the plus side, you have recovered a big haul of firearms and drugs.'

'True. To hear Garwood telling Sir Barnaby, you'd think he did the whole thing single-handedly. The National Crime Agency is well pleased.' He picked some pieces of chestnut out of his teeth. 'But they're saying what they really need is evidence that ties The Bard indisputably to the actual procurement and trading in illegal imports. It's all very well being able to prove that the heads of organized crime have given him a great deal of money, but they're not going to come forward and say what they were expecting to get for it, are they? At the moment, Bernie's stonewalling — giving me a load of old cobblers about not knowing the stuff was in his strongroom, blaming his wife for setting him up. She's living in Sicily with her family who sound even dodgier than the Shakespeares.'

'When will Bernie be fit enough to be questioned again?' Corrie wondered.

'I've no idea. And anyway, as head of MIT, my main responsibility is to charge Marco for the murders of Venetia Adler and your ex-hubby, and I'm almost there. The laboratory has found traces of Tom's blood on the knife that we took from Marco when he was arrested. All I need to do now is inform him and avocado-lady that his alibi for that night has been discredited and with any luck, it'll shock him into confessing to strangling Venetia. He's pretty volatile at the best of times.'

Corrie busied herself loading the dishwasher. She tried not to look Jack in the eye, while choosing her words carefully. 'Suppose the NCA had access to Bernie's original plan — you know, maps, the route that the shipment took, who the suppliers were, lists of names, stuff like that?'

'Well, that would be amazing but his laptop and all the other devices in the house were destroyed by the fire. Where else are they going to get that kind of information?'

'Have you searched the Tempest Club?'

'Uniform have been all over it ever since it closed. They found plenty of evidence of prostitution, money laundering, protection — all the usual unpleasant activities of criminal gangs, but nothing about illegal imports. Why do you ask?'

'Tell them to try the boardroom. It's on the ground floor behind a door marked "Private. Strictly No Entry". There's a big oval table like the ones they have in company confer- ences. It looks perfectly ordinary, but if you press a button sunk into the underside of one end, a device like a gaming console rises up out of the top. The controller is connected to a screen on the wall with video and audio output. Carlene hit a few buttons and got the whole shooting match — times, names, locations, an audio inventory of the merchandise — the lot. And I'll bet you'll find Jonnie's prints on it, too, so he can't say he didn't know anything about it.'

Jack's eyebrows shot up. 'What the hell was Carlene doing there?'

'She picked the lock so we could get in.'

He took her by the shoulders and turned her to face him. 'Corrie, what have you been up to?'

She prevaricated. 'It was a girls' night out.'

'What girls?'

'Carlene, Cynthia and me.' Corrie could see no reason to get Gemma and Velma into trouble. 'We thought we'd go to a club and we happened upon the video thingy entirely by accident.'

'No, you didn't!' Jack countered. 'How could it have been an accident if you had to pick the lock to get in? It was the three C's again, wasn't it? And you were snooping. Corrie, this isn't a video game. These men are dangerous. People have gone into that club and come out feet first.'

Corrie smiled to herself. It was true. They'd manoeuvred Cynthia out through the window feet first, but she didn't reckon Jack was in the mood to find it amusing.

'What were you thinking?' Jack groaned in despair.

'I was thinking that if I couldn't find some evidence to link Marco Shakespeare to Tom's murder, Crump was going to fit me up for it and I'd spend the next several years cooking porridge in a prison kitchen.'

Jack put his arms around her and hugged her tight. 'Do you think I'd have let that happen, you daft bat? If anything happened to you, I don't know what I'd do.'

'I know exactly what you'd do. You'd live on corned beef hash and baked beans.'

'And brown sauce, sweetheart. Don't forget the brown sauce.'

* * *

Despite his concerns for Corrie, Jack had to admit that it was a good lead. He passed the information to his contact in the NCA and they immediately arranged a thorough search. Jack had planned to go with them, but DCS Garwood decided that he and Jack should visit DI Crump in hospital. He was, after all, on loan from another division and George didn't want accusations of failing in his duty of care. They found Percy sitting up in bed covered in bandages and sticking plaster.

'How are you, Crumpet old man?' Garwood asked, affably.

'Pretty pissed off, if you want the truth, sir. The doctor said if I hadn't been in the khazi when the bomb went off, I'd probably be dead. As it is, they're still picking bits of porcelain out of my behind. Have you arrested Teresa Shakespeare?'

'On what charge?' asked Garwood, puzzled.

'Assault. She hit me over the head with a hippopotamus.'

George took Jack to one side and whispered, 'Is he still concussed, do you think?'

Jack furrowed his brow. 'It's hard to tell with DI Crump, sir. I shouldn't be at all surprised.'

'Well, don't you worry, Crumpet.' Garwood patted his hand. 'You just stay there and rest until you're better. Then we'll get you back to Q Division.'

They went outside into the corridor. 'While we're here, sir, I think I'll just check how Bernie Shakespeare's doing.'

'Yes, I heard about that. Some sort of fracas with his son while they were both in police custody, wasn't it? Tread carefully, Dawes. We don't want any accusations of negligence.'

They walked down the corridor to Bernie's private room. The bed was empty and his possessions had gone.

'Looks like he's been discharged and transferred back to the station, sir.' Jack looked around for the uniformed constable who'd been guarding him, but he wasn't on the door. 'I should be able to start questioning him again soon.'

A nurse appeared in the doorway. 'Are you relatives of Mr Shakespeare?'

'No,' Jack replied. 'We're police officers. Do you know when he left?'

'In a manner of speaking. He died an hour ago. He's been taken to the mortuary. I understand Doctor Hardacre will be performing the post-mortem.' She bustled away.

Jack and Garwood exchanged glances. 'This is a bad business, Dawes.' Garwood was already imagining all kinds of consequences that might find him culpable of something and working out how he could avoid them. 'Sort it out.'

* * *

There were no surprises in Bernie Shakespeare's post-mortem report. Big Ron had recorded cause of death as a massive myocardial infarction brought on by a traumatic event. He was, she pointed out, in very poor physical shape to start with. Overweight, lungs full of poison from smoking, too much alcohol, high cholesterol, type-two diabetes, a liver that looked like an old dishcloth and too little exercise. He was, in fact, a heart attack looking for somewhere to happen and that somewhere turned out to be the corridor in the custody suite following a physical attack by his son. Apart from a few awkward questions as to how the attack was able to happen in a police station, there was nothing left for the coroner to question.

News of The Bard's death spread through the under-world like chicken pox at a children's party. All the wannabee successors to his throne were getting their ducks in a row before staking a claim. Demonstrations of power had been hampered since they had neither the firearms nor the drugs they had banked on to bolster their claims. And however aggrieved they felt, they were hardly in a position to sue Bernie's estate for their money back. Nevertheless, a good deal of sabre-rattling went on. With both Shakespeare sons in police custody and likely to remain there, the sovereignty of the man who was "too big to bring down" was up for grabs.

Underworld bookmakers were taking bets with Charlie Fraser as odds-on favourite. Frankie Silver and Vinnie the Vic running at ten-to-one, Billy "Biscuit" McVitie and Mick "the Miller" both at fifteen-to-one, while Semtex Sid had dropped to a hundred-to-one due to his failed attempt to steal the entire consignment which, had it been successful, would have pushed him way up the field. What they hadn't taken into account was that thanks to the sterling snooping of the fearless five and, it has to be said, a fair bit of luck, the NCA had what they needed to take many syndicates out of circulation for at least the next few years. It was open season and many also-rans were sharpening their knives, but it would be a long time before such a powerful network of crime would be established again.

* * *

If Jack expected Marco to display any grief when he was told his father was dead, he was disappointed.

'It's karma,' he declared. 'Punishment for forcing himself on Venetia and lying about it — saying she was willing. She was my woman, she belonged to me. It's all his fault that she's dead.'

'Do you want to tell me about that, Marco?' Jack asked.

'Not really.'

Miss Timms leaned across and whispered in his ear at some length. She was dressed differently today — a patchwork poncho over an ankle-length vintage-print dress and biker boots. As well as rows of clinking beads, she wore huge Bohemian earrings — a silver sun on one ear and a celestial moonstone on the other. 'I have advised my client that since the crown has irrefutable forensic evidence that the blood on his knife belongs to a murdered man, he should make a statement explaining what happened on the night in question and ask for his cooperation to be taken into account.'

'Is that right, sir?' asked Bugsy.

'Yeah, I guess so. You'll find out anyway. Me and Ven were meant to be going to Papà's birthday party but when I went to find her, she was still in her pyjamas. I asked her what was wrong and she said she felt sick and wouldn't be able to eat party food nor drink alcohol. She'd had a chicken salad for supper and now she was going to bed. I asked her if she needed a doctor and she laughed and said no, it was quite normal to feel sick in her condition. Well, I was over the moon. I said we should get married — another Shakespeare in line to take over the business. That's when she told me it wasn't mine. I asked her whose it was and she wouldn't tell me. That's when I thought it was Jonnie and I must have lost it because I grabbed her round the throat and shook her.'

'What happened then?' Jack decided that up to this point, Marco might just have got away with voluntary manslaughter. It was what he did afterwards that would get him a life sentence.

'She was screaming and fighting me, then she went limp. I turned around and this bloke was standing there. He'd broken in, intending to nick stuff I suppose. Anyway, he legged it and triggered the alarms and the guards went after him. Well, I couldn't let him get away, could I? Not after what he'd seen. Me and the lads cornered him in the underpass and I phoned Papà. He said to take him back to the house, but he escaped again so I had to shiv him.'

'Shivved means that he . . .' began Miss Timms.

'Thank you, Miss, we know what it means,' said Bugsy. 'Then you put his body in the back of a van with Coriander's Cuisine on the side.'

'If you say so.' He shrugged. 'It was green and full of pots and pans and kitchen junk. I saw a knife and I thought it would be a clever idea to stick it in the same place where I'd pulled mine out. Then we went home.'

Bugsy thought he'd heard it all from punks like this kid, but this was something else. No flicker of guilt, remorse, regret or emotion. Young Velma would have a name for it

— psycho something or other. He was that, all right. But whatever they called it, Marco Shakespeare was destined to a life of incarceration for the foreseeable future. No more fast cars and beautiful women. Just where that incarceration might take place was a matter of conjecture according to DC Fox. She believed that with a good barrister, the court might dismiss *mens rea* and accept medical evidence that he was "unfit to plead". He could end up with a hospital order.

'What happened to Venetia Adler's body?' asked Jack.

Marco looked at Miss Timms and she nodded. 'Grant took care of her. It was one of his jobs — getting rid of bodies. I think she ended up on a farm somewhere.' He sniggered. 'Maybe he put her in the pigsty — they'll eat anything.'

Jack had had enough. 'Stand up, please, Mr Shakespeare.' He charged him with both murders, cautioned him and two uniformed constables led him away in handcuffs.

Miss Timms shoved her laptop into a voluminous hessian bag on top of what looked like a bunch of kale. 'Do you ever wonder, Inspector Dawes, how such a superficially attractive young man can be so inherently ugly?'

'Not really, Miss Timms. Not anymore.'

* * *

'Jack, there's a Mr and Mrs Bell on the desk, wanting to see you.' Sergeant Parsloe intercepted Dawes and Bugsy on their way back to the incident room.

'Do you know what it's about, Norman, only I've got a mountain of reports to write. Couldn't Aled or Gemma deal with it?'

'They say it's about their daughter, Tracey, and they've come a long way. Glasgow, I believe they said. And they particularly wanted to talk to you.'

'OK, put them in an interview room and give them some tea and I'll be there as soon as I can.'

'Do we know anything about this young woman?' Jack asked Bugsy.

'Don't think so, guv. Doesn't ring any bells.' He chuckled. 'Did you see what I did there?'

'Just for that awful pun, you can come with me to talk to them.

Jimmy and Maggie Bell looked tired and anxious, as if they hadn't slept for a week. They stood up when Jack and Bugsy came in but Jack waved them back down.

'Please sit down. I'm Detective Inspector Dawes and this is Detective Sergeant Malone. How can we help you?'

They looked at each other, unsure where to start. 'We live in Glasgow, Mr Dawes, and until about a year ago, our Tracey lived there too,' Maggie began.

'After she left school, she couldn't seem to settle. She had a job on the checkout in the local supermarket, but she was bored, she said, and wanted something more exciting.' Maggie took out a tissue and dabbed her eyes.

'You'd think a city like Glasgow would be exciting enough for anyone, but no, Tracey wanted to live in London,' Jimmy said. 'She spent all her free time surfing the internet for pictures and jobs and she said London was where it was all "happening".'

'So, one day, she drew out all her savings and off she went. Just like that.' Maggie was clearly heartbroken.

'If you're here to report her missing, Mrs Bell, you need a different police department,' advised Jack. 'We're from the Murder Investigation Team.'

'We know,' said Jimmy. 'Please bear with us. We're getting to why we've come here. Tracey used to message her mother regularly, because she knew how she worried. She said she'd found a job, a good one, well paid and with prospects. She was keen to emphasise the prospects.'

'When I asked her where she was working, she sent me this picture.' Maggie took out her phone, scrolled through until she found and passed it to Jack. It was a picture of the front entrance of the Tempest Club at night.

With the lights and people queueing to go in, it looked, Jack thought, quite the place to be if you were young, looking for excitement and didn't know what the club was really like. 'How old is Tracey, Mrs Bell?'

'She turned nineteen last week. We'd have sent a card but we didn't have her address. She told us she moved around a lot and it was better to stick to messaging.'

'Anyway, Inspector, to cut a long story short,' said Jimmy, 'a couple of months ago, she told us she was engaged to the son of the owner of the club but said it was only "a means to an end". We didn't really understand what she meant.'

'We thought she'd landed on her feet. She sounded happy. Then the messages stopped.' Maggie sniffed.

'A neighbour of ours who moved to this area with his job a couple of years ago, saw this article in the *Richington Echo* and sent us the newspaper cutting.' Jimmy took out his wallet and pulled out a piece of paper. He passed it over and Bugsy stared hard, then gave it to Jack who read it.

> *Fred Lynch, 45, was shot dead on his own doorstep in what is thought to be a revenge killing. This follows the recent discovery of the murdered body of Venetia Adler on the farm where Lynch worked.*

'Our neighbour recognized her straightaway from this newspaper photo even though he hadn't seen her for a couple of years. It says her name is Venetia Adler, but it's our Tracey.'

'The article says her body has been found — murdered.' Maggie's voice trembled.

'Is it true, Inspector Dawes?' asked Jimmy. 'Is our girl dead?'

Jack and Bugsy exchanged glances. They'd been present when Venetia- alias-Tracey had been uncovered on top of the silage mound and at her post-mortem. There was no mistake.

Jack hated these situations when he had to pass on terrible news to decent, loving parents. Worse still, they'd have to be told that Tracey had been pregnant, but not right now. They had enough to cope with. 'I'm so sorry, Mr and Mrs

Bell, but if this newspaper photo is your daughter, then I'm very much afraid that she is dead.'

Maggie had been trying hard not to cry, but it was too much and she burst into floods of tears. Jimmy put his arm around her. 'Do you think we could see her?'

'Yes, of course. We'll arrange a proper identification, then when Tracey's body is released, you can make the funeral arrangements,' Bugsy assured him.

On their way back upstairs in the lift, Jack and Bugsy were unusually sombre and lost in their own thoughts, until Bugsy said, 'What do you think Venetia — I mean, Tracey — meant by saying her engagement to Marco was only "a means to an end"?'

'I guess we'll never know, but a cynical person might suggest that her sights were set on Bernie all along. She used Marco to wheedle her way first into the club and then into the house.'

'You reckon she wanted a baby by the organ grinder, not the monkey?'

'That's right. As she saw it, a child by Bernie would have ensured her a place in the powerful and wealthy Shakespeare dynasty. I doubt if that would have happened with Marco.'

CHAPTER TWENTY

When they reached the incident room, Aled was cleaning the storyboard with vigour. 'Good result, eh, sir? A confession to both murders from Marco and the CPS have approved charges of accessory, compliance, joint enterprise, perverting the course and trading in illegal arms against Jonnie Shakespeare, and that's just for a start. Are we going to celebrate in the pub?'

'Not quite yet, Aled. There's still the matter of the man who disposed of Venetia Adler's body on Bert Cook's silage, and incidentally, her real name was Tracey Bell. When I asked Marco Shakespeare, he said "Grant took care of her". We know Fred Lynch helped and they put out a contract to silence him.

'And Joe, the bouncer from the Tempest Club, came in to tell us that he saw Grant, Bernie's right-hand man, in the pub with Semtex Sid on several occasions, hatching a plot,' recalled Bugsy.

'Why would they plot to blow up Bernie's house with all that valuable loot in it?' asked Aled.

'Maybe it was a plot that went wrong,' suggested Gemma. 'We know that Bernie treated Grant like a skivvy, according to Joe. Maybe he was fed up with it and thought he deserved a proper stake in the business. He was never going to get it with two sons waiting to take over, so he teamed up with Sid who wanted to add Bernie's criminal empire to his own.'

'Clive, what do we know about this Grant fellow?' asked Jack.

'I've got several aliases for him. He fell off the DWP and HMRC radars after his last stretch inside when he seems to have taken the rap for a nasty GBH that Bernie did. The bloke had both his legs broken with a hammer. As for an address, I've drawn a blank after the Tempest Club.'

'Maybe he has a bedsit in there somewhere,' offered Gemma.

'If he had, wouldn't uniform have found it?' asked Jack. 'They've been all over that place.'

'Maybe they did find it but didn't realize what it was. If it was just a room with a bed, bottles and glasses, they might have just assumed it was used by the call girls who worked there.'

'That's a good point, Gemma. I'll get them to take another look. We need to catch this guy before he slips through the net.'

* * *

Up in his crow's nest of a bedsit in the eaves of the club, Grant was getting his few possessions together. Over time, he'd found it advisable to travel light, never knowing when he'd have to move on and often with little warning. Bernie was dead — he wouldn't shed any tears. He had been The Bard's enforcer-in-chief for a long time, doing all the messy jobs with little appreciation or reward. His proposed alliance with Sid wasn't going to happen now that the Semtex supremo was inside awaiting his sentence. He wondered, with hindsight, exactly how much of an expert Sid had been. For a start, there had been way too much explosive just to blow open a strongroom door. It had taken off the whole roof of Bernie's house. And how had the burner phone that he had attached so carefully to the door hinge of the club's vault transferred to Bernie's strongroom? He'd probably never know. And that was another thing — why hadn't Bernie taken him into his confidence and told him he'd moved the stuff? He guessed it didn't matter now. He was off to somewhere warm — new name, new start. He had a bit put by for such an occasion and he'd still got Venetia's jewellery that he'd taken off her before they buried her under the tarpaulin. It was good stuff and should be worth a fair bit. And he'd soon find a job that matched his talents. Crime was rife wherever you went, if you knew where to look.

He had a brief glance around to make sure he hadn't left anything behind, then picked up his backpack and threw it over his shoulder. When he opened the door and looked down the spiral staircase, he could see two uniformed officers coming up the first flight. If he didn't want to meet them head on, he had only one option. He went back inside, opened the window and climbed out onto the roof, intending to conceal himself there until they'd gone. The club had been built in the early twentieth century as a gentlemen's club and it was doubtful whether any significant maintenance on the roof had been done since, but there were chimneys he could hide behind. This was the second time the coppers had searched the place so Grant doubted they'd bother coming right to the top. He was wrong. Moments later, a head appeared through the window and the constable spotted him.

'Come along, now, sir. There's nowhere to go. Come back inside. It isn't safe.'

There was just one chance. On the other side of the building, there was a ladder that, years ago, had once seen service as a fire escape. It was attached to the wall, with the last few feet constructed so that it would slide down from above to prevent people from climbing up it. Grant thought fast. If he could get across the roof, he could be down and away before the coppers knew he'd gone. He picked his way carefully across the elderly slate tiles which cracked and splintered under his feet. Nearly there. He threw his backpack over the edge then tried one foot on the top of the ladder. It felt fairly sound so he climbed down a couple of rungs. Creaking and grinding under his weight, it broke free from the wall with a crack. For desperate moments, Grant swung outwards, suspended in mid-air, until he lost his grip and plummeted to the ground.

When the police officers reached him, they could tell straight away that he was dead. His neck was broken and his head, lying in a pool of blood, was at an unnatural angle to his body.

* * *

'As a way of tying up loose ends, that was a bit extreme,' observed Corrie. 'What an awful way to go, poor chap.' It was two days before Christmas and she had finally got around to putting up the decorations. The living room was festooned with twinkling lights and she was draping holly and ivy garlands along the mantelpiece. She had long since given up on hanging mistletoe over the doorway as Jack always hit his head on it every time he walked through.

Jack was struggling down the loft ladder with the tree. 'I don't know about "poor chap".' Wheezing, he plonked it down in the hall and it promptly fell over. 'Grant was responsible for illegally disposing of countless bodies for Bernie, including Venetia Adler's. Hiring a sniper to take out Fred Lynch was just another day at the office for him. He did it without any qualms about Fred's wife and kids. Grant had choices in life, like the rest of us, and he chose to work for a particularly violent and vicious criminal.'

'Still, with Bernie dead and his cronies on their way to a long spell in the nick, the air will be a little fresher. I heard that the NCA is taking out court orders to cripple their criminal empires by seizing their cash and ill-gotten gains.'

'Hmm.' Jack was doubtful. 'Gangsters are like hydra. You cut off one head and two more grow in its place. We may have slowed down the decay, but we'll never put a stop to it.'

'Since they pulled down the remains of "New Place", the look and the atmosphere of Eden Park has changed drastically. Bernie's hefty, ferocious security guards have all drifted away, and now the place is watched over by a firm called "Safe Haven". They're paid for out of the residents' maintenance charges.'

'Sounds a bit soft for a team of security guards.' Jack was unconvinced.

'That's because they're all ladies. They wear pale-blue uniforms with hi-vis waistcoats and stewardess hats. They look so smart and professional compared to the last lot. Maurice loves them. They look in on him when they're patrolling to make sure he's OK.'

'Yes, I'm sure they look lovely, but what are they like in a tough situation?'

'Tough, of course! What did you think? They have iron fists in velvet gloves — they don't tolerate trouble. Unlike me. I have chapped fists in rubber gloves and I live with trouble all the time.'

'That's because you're always looking for it. I worry constantly about what you're going to do next.'

'I was thinking of making some mulled wine, actually.'

'Good idea.'

* * *

The editor of the *Echo* was uncharacteristically subtle when printing The Bard's obituary. It would obviously have been inappropriate to have extolled his perceived virtues in light of what had been revealed about him after his death. Hidden beneath the charity donations and the village cricket matches, his life had been one of crime, violence and flagrant disregard of law and order. Since neither of his sons chose to come out of prison to attend his funeral, it was a police officer who followed the coffin to the crematorium. Bernie Shakespeare's obituary consisted of one line:

> *Exit, pursued by a bear. (Act lll The Winter's Tale. William Shakespeare)*

THE END

THE JOFFE BOOKS STORY

We began in 2014 when Jasper agreed to publish his mum's much-rejected romance novel and it became a bestseller.

Since then we've grown into the largest independent publisher in the UK. We're extremely proud to publish some of the very best writers in the world, including Joy Ellis, Faith Martin, Caro Ramsay, Helen Forrester, Simon Brett and Robert Goddard. Everyone at Joffe Books loves reading and we never forget that it all begins with the magic of an author telling a story.

We are proud to publish talented first-time authors, as well as established writers whose books we love introducing to a new generation of readers.

We have been shortlisted for Independent Publisher of the Year at the British Book Awards three times, in 2020, 2021 and 2022, and for the Diversity and Inclusivity Award at the Independent Publishing Awards in 2022.

We built this company with your help, and we love to hear from you, so please email us about absolutely anything bookish at feedback@joffebooks.com

If you want to receive free books every Friday and hear about all our new releases, join our mailing list: www.joffebooks.com/contact

And when you tell your friends about us, just remember: it's pronounced Joffe as in coffee or toffee!

Milton Keynes UK
Ingram Content Group UK Ltd.
UKHW010253221123
432980UK00005B/349

9 781835 262375